"Freeze!"

The attacker stumbled away and then picked up speed.

Growling, Everly started after him, but Sawyer grabbed her arm.

She yanked her arm free. "Let me go! I need to get him."

"Layla." He said the one word, the name. The reason he'd hired Everly.

She stopped in her tracks.

They could both run after this guy, but he doubted they would find him tonight in the dark. Sawyer couldn't leave Everly alone to find the guy, but neither could he leave his niece alone.

"Why did you leave her?" She sent him an accusing look.

He fisted his hands at his sides. "Someone was attacking you!"

"Someone say my name?" The young voice bounced against the trees dripping with rain.

And Layla stepped up behind Sawyer.

"What are you doing here?" he huffed out, failing to hide his frustration. "You should have stayed in the house."

She seemed oblivious to what happened around her most of the time, always on her cell. He hadn't stopped to think she might come looking for them. He'd only thought to save Everly.

Elizabeth Goddard is the award-winning author of more than thirty novels and novellas. A 2011 Carol Award winner, she was a double finalist in the 2016 Daphne du Maurier Award for Excellence in Mystery/Suspense and a 2016 Carol Award finalist. Elizabeth graduated with a computer science degree and worked in high-level software sales before retiring to write full-time.

Books by Elizabeth Goddard

Love Inspired Suspense

Honor Protection Specialists

Mount Shasta Secrets

Coldwater Bay Intrigue

Rocky Mountain K-9 Unit

Visit the Author Profile page at LoveInspired.com for more titles.

PERILOUS
SECURITY DETAIL

ELIZABETH
GODDARD

LOVE INSPIRED SUSPENSE
INSPIRATIONAL ROMANCE

LOVE INSPIRED SUSPENSE
INSPIRATIONAL ROMANCE

ISBN-13: 978-1-335-58759-6

Perilous Security Detail

For questions and comments about the quality of this book, please contact us
at CustomerService@Harlequin.com.

Love Inspired
22 Adelaide St. West, 41st Floor
Toronto, Ontario M5H 4E3, Canada
www.LoveInspired.com

Printed in U.S.A.

Recycling programs
for this product may
not exist in your area.

Be not afraid, only believe.
—*Mark* 5:36

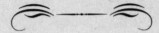

ONE

October; Puget Sound

The familiar sensation of being watched swept over Sawyer Blackwood as he set fresh roses on the pedestal of the tombstone for his twin sister, Paisley. Like he'd done every year for the past four years. This was the anniversary of her death, after all. Her murder.

He read the epitaph:

Life is not about waiting for the storm to pass. It's about learning how to dance in the rain.

It was, in fact, raining both literally and in a metaphorical sense… "I'm trying to dance in the rain, sis."

But dancing in the rain held an entirely different meaning for him these days. His sister had perhaps danced in the rain during the storm, but she hadn't lived through it, and he came back every year to remind himself that he could have made a difference if he hadn't been overseas. He came back to her grave every year to remind himself why he was involved in his particular clandestine operation.

Water droplets clung to the rose petals before dripping off. "Don't worry, sis. I'll keep her safe."

When he could no longer ignore the prickle of his skin,

the raised hair on the back of his neck, he lifted his gaze from the roses and tombstone and glanced around the cemetery, which consisted of several acres of rolling hills, groomed lawn and aesthetically placed trees, views of Puget Sound, and the Olympic Mountains in the distance—peaceful scenery, really, except that he knew someone had followed him here and was watching his every move. But Sawyer didn't see anyone hiding behind a tree or standing at another gravesite, pretending to visit a loved one while watching him. On such a dreary day, he only spotted an elderly couple standing under a red umbrella at a gravesite.

He turned his back on the tombstone to return to his vehicle. Across the cemetery and by the main building, he caught sight of a blue Cadillac sedan with dark windows—the same one he'd seen last night. He'd been unable to retrieve the license plate number, but maybe today he could remedy that. Sawyer was wearing a raincoat, but he didn't pull the hood up over his head, nor did he carry an umbrella. Living in the Puget Sound region had made him used to the rain. He walked up the hill and was almost breathless by the time he got to his white GMC Acadia. He remained aware of his surroundings, and in his peripheral vision, he could still see the Cadillac as he shrugged out of his raincoat before climbing into his vehicle.

So far, the Cadillac had remained in place. As he exited the cemetery, Sawyer kept to a normal speed and hoped the Cadillac's driver would catch up to him or get close enough that he could see and memorize the license plate number. For all he knew, someone could have been following him for days and he had just failed to notice earlier.

Regardless, as soon as he'd spotted the tail last night, he'd contacted a security service and requested protection for his niece, Layla, for whom he was now guardian after his sister's death. Some might think his actions hasty, but he refused to hesitate like his father had years ago. His inaction had precipitated unnecessary trauma for Sawyer and Paisley.

Finally, he spotted the Cadillac in his rearview mirror; it was following him, keeping three cars behind. That was too far for him to see who was driving or catch the license plate. Now he wished that he had simply walked up to the car and faced off with the driver while at the cemetery. Get it over with because right now, he couldn't know with certainty from where his troubles stemmed.

The present.

The recent past.

Or the distant past.

Any trouble could be dangerous for him, his niece and his clients.

He approached a traffic light and slowed through the green, knowing the follower wouldn't make it through the light, and he *needed* them to follow him. He almost chuckled at the idea that he was letting them follow, willing them to get closer. Usually, people tried to escape their abusers and stalkers. He knew all about it.

A loud honk drew his attention to the right.

The grille of a Mack truck filled the window, filled his vision, a nightmare waiting to happen. Panic swelled in his chest as every fear he'd ever had seemed to culminate in that one moment. It was true that life passed before your eyes moments before you died.

Or at least, before your mind thought you were going to die.

Sawyer had no time to react as the honking blared in his ears. In reflex, he squeezed his eyes shut, managing a thousand prayers for help in one millisecond of time, and he threw his arms up over his head as the truck slammed into his vehicle at full force like a train barreling forward, jarring him to his bones. Both frontal and side-impact airbags exploded, and the seat belt pinned him in place as the vehicle rolled down an incline.

Over and over.

Then flipped one last time, landing right side up. The Acadia shook, the vibrations shuddering through his core.

He gasped for breath and opened his eyes.

Am I still alive? He sat in stunned silence. Everything had happened in mere moments but felt like time had slowed.

Sawyer had to get his bearings. Catch his breath. Get out of this vehicle. But the door would not budge.

Smoke filled the cab of the Acadia, and flames crackled and hissed.

He was going to die—and if he died, who would keep Layla safe?

Everly Honor pulled over to the shoulder and jumped out. She raced toward the vehicle she'd watched get slammed by the truck and roll several times down the incline. If that wasn't bad enough, now it had gone up in flames.

Heart racing, she skidded to a stop close to the vehicle and spotted the driver. He was alive and trying to escape. She had to pull him out and make sure no one else was in the SUV.

"God, please let them all be alive. Help them to get out."

She couldn't bear the horror of what she was seeing, nor would she stand by and simply watch, like other onlookers up the hill who were capturing video with their cell phones.

What do I do? What do I do?

What was the best way into the vehicle, the best escape path?

Flames crawled around the edges and over the door, and would soon reach the gas tank—and when that happened, the vehicle would explode. She had seconds to rescue the man; he had seconds to live if she failed. Smoke was rapidly filling the cab of the vehicle, which could kill him just as quickly.

She yanked off her jacket and wrapped it around her arm and hand, then grabbed the door handle. The man inside rammed his shoulder against the door panel as she continued to pull.

"The frame must have gotten damaged!" she shouted.

He nodded. Through the haze, she saw him cover his face with his arm and shift over to the passenger seat. He lifted his legs and started kicking at the window. She backed away, praying for his success as she watched the flames grow angry and aggressive.

How much longer before they breached the gas tank?

He kicked again, hard, and the glass shattered, already weakened from the multiple impacts that had damaged the chassis. Everly rushed forward and used her jacket to clear out the glass in the window's frame; then she pressed it along the ledge. He crawled out, slipping onto the ground, coughing and hacking. He rolled onto his back and glanced over at his vehicle.

"Is there anyone else inside?" she asked.

Coughing, he shook his head. Good to know.

"We have to get to safety. Come on!" She might have to drag him away in case the flames reached the gas tank.

He barely scrambled to his feet and stumbled as he walked. He leaned on her as she led him to a large tree a safe distance from the burning vehicle. Then she settled him on the ground against the trunk to watch the display, along with the rest of the world via the images recorded by all the people on the street above.

"Are you hurt? Are you okay?"

He groaned and pressed his hands against his temples and shook his head. "I'm good. The airbags..." He glanced up at her with dark brown eyes.

And recognition dawned in those familiar eyes as well as in her heart.

"Sawyer? Sawyer...*Blackwood*?"

"Everly... Thank you for helping me." Sawyer coughed against his sleeve. He was wearing a white button-down shirt and dress slacks—professional attire—that were covered in black smudges from the smoke and flames.

"I'm so glad I was there to help—but in the end, you got yourself out of the car."

The sound of rushing water from a fire hose drew their attention. The sirens had resounded in the background, but she'd been too busy to notice that help had arrived. The firemen wore full protective fire-resistant clothing and self-contained breathing apparatuses—even for a car fire. She glanced back at Sawyer.

You're fortunate to be alive.

He had the same strong jaw she remembered. Strong and angular, with a bit of scruff covering his olive complexion. With his dark hair and eyes and strong features, he definitely had a Mediterranean look.

He dropped his head and closed his eyes. "Looks like my car is toast. Literally."

The ambulance maneuvered along the road, and people parted to let it through. It parked a safe distance from the vehicle fire, which was nearly extinguished. EMTs jumped out, grabbed a gurney and then wheeled it down the incline toward the tree where Everly and Sawyer waited.

"Sawyer, they're here for you."

He lifted his face and his frown deepened; then he tried to push to his feet.

She tugged him back down. "No, you don't. You've been in an accident. The EMTs are on the way to you." She waved to urge them to hurry.

That's when she saw the man from the alley again. Only this time, he was standing in the shadows by the trees at the bottom of the hill, watching. Considering a lot of other people had stopped to watch, it wasn't anything out of the ordinary, at least on the surface. But there was something in the way he crossed his arms, the set of his shoulders and overall demeanor...

And the fact that she'd seen him *before* the accident.

Standing there waiting, as if he expected it to happen. *Wanted* it to happen.

She'd been sitting at a red light when she saw him, and she grew suspicious.

Was she letting her imagination get the best of her?

Everly stepped out of the way as the EMTs assisted Sawyer onto the gurney. He rested his head against the slim mattress and squeezed his eyes shut. Poor Sawyer. She could only imagine how shaken he must be after being hit so hard, and then his vehicle rolling. He'd almost been burned alive. Her hands shook and she'd only been watching.

The EMTs pushed the gurney up the incline—no easy task—and she followed and caught up.

She took Sawyer's hand, and he squeezed back, his grip strong and sure, if not a little shaky.

"I'll go with you. Is there anyone I can call for you?"

"No," he said.

The answer sent pain through her heart. He had no one she could call? Everly and Sawyer had dated back in their early college years, and she could have seen a future with him—except then, a tragedy struck his family, and after the proverbial dust settled, Sawyer and his twin sister, Paisley, had simply fallen off the face of the earth—intentionally.

The EMTs pushed him into the ambulance, and she rushed to her vehicle. Now that she thought about it, maybe his negative response had been to tell her he didn't want her to go with him or to meet him at the hospital. But she was going.

She followed the ambulance to the local hospital and parked in guest parking, then rushed in as the gurney transported him down the hall and into the emergency department. Everly kept pace with the hospital staff like she had every right to be there. She'd been a police officer in the past and now worked security services, and she knew how to present herself so that she wouldn't be questioned.

The EMTs knew she'd been with him at the car-crash site and might assume that she was with him—as in, *with* him. She had been *with* him at one time…until he broke her heart when he left without so much as a goodbye.

While having Everly's familiar face by his side had been reassuring in the literal heat of the moment as she'd helped him out of the burning car; offered her assistance in his life-and-death battle; and then, finally, rushed with him to receive emergency services, he wasn't sure why she'd been there in the first place. Or why she was still here now, sitting in the chair while he rested on the bed in a private room in the emergency department.

Sawyer had been treated for a burn on his hand and a small cut on his temple. The pain didn't bother him, especially in light of the fact that the accident could have been much worse. The terror of it remained, though, and if he closed his eyes, he could see the big truck barreling toward him, the heat and smoke of the flames increasing. The fire was extinguished before it had reached the gas tank, for which he was grateful.

Why hadn't the truck put on the brakes? It seemed like it had sped up instead of trying to stop. Had the incident been an accident…or intentional? He'd given his statement to the police officer who'd come to the hospital room. Maybe focusing on his tail was what had led to the accident; he hadn't paid enough attention to the road. But unfortunately, he didn't think that was it, because he'd been the one with the green light.

Or had it turned? He couldn't remember exactly now.

He groaned inwardly and squeezed his eyes shut—but then quickly regretted closing them when the images bombarded him again. He'd talked to the police officer and suggested the truck had run a red light. But since Sawyer was overly suspicious and too cautious, he hadn't mentioned to the officer that he believed the accident had been intentional on the truck driver's part. Let them come to that conclusion on their own.

His biggest fear—his twelve-year-old niece, Layla, could be in danger, and Sawyer didn't have time to sit in the hospital. He reined in the anxiety coursing through him and glanced at his watch. He had two hours before he had to pick Layla up from school, so he had time. Sawyer had promised her that he would pick her up so that she wouldn't have to be embarrassed when the bouncer-looking bodyguard he'd hired showed up at school. He was beginning to wonder why he'd even hired the guy; then again he appreciated having extra protection for Layla, just in case. She had been incensed at what she called Sawyer's "overreach."

He was her guardian, after all, and the responsibility to make sure she was safe and well cared for fell on his shoulders. Even if he hadn't been named guardian, he loved Layla and would bear the responsibility anyway. As for his hospital stay, whether he was officially released or not, he had every intention of leaving in the next few minutes.

Everly's sharp hazel eyes glanced from her cell phone to him, and she didn't seem to miss a thing. Now her presence in his room was starting to make things a bit awkward. He hadn't forgotten her beautiful eyes, serious expression or the way she put her whole heart into everything. She wore her silky brown hair shorter now— shoulder length, rather than long layers that hung to her waist. Hair he'd once loved to weave his fingers through. Either way, she still looked good to him. He shoved those thoughts to the back of his mind.

Sawyer sat up. He was bandaged and stitched, and it was time to go. "You don't have to stay with me, you know."

Pursing her lips, she furrowed her brows, but he caught the hint of a smile behind her eyes. "Don't I? Sawyer, you were just in a wreck. You were almost killed and... I saw the whole thing." Her voice grew thick with emotion. "If there's someone else you'd prefer at your side, then by all means, call them and I'll leave." Then she leveled her gaze at him—so familiar, so... *Ah, Everly, I missed you!* "Or is it me? You just don't want me in the room with you?"

Now that he thought about it, he wouldn't have anyone else here with him, but he couldn't tell her that.

Still, he couldn't help but smile because Everly Honor had a special way about her that lit up the dark places inside him. "Of course it's not you." His words brought back a rush of memories from years ago, when he and

Everly had been together. He hadn't meant to disappear, to leave her behind so spectacularly.

I never forgot you.

Since then, Sawyer had become very intentional regarding everything he did, but seeing Everly sitting in the chair—in his life, however briefly—reminded him that God had a reason for everything He did too. Or maybe Sawyer was reading too much into it. He hadn't intended to end up nearly dying today, so that was also a reminder that he didn't have full control over his life, no matter how intentional he thought he was. Still, he wished that he hadn't left his relationship with her as unfinished business. He'd wanted to communicate with her, but he and Paisley had their reasons for leaving—at least, for a time.

Crossing her legs, Everly sat back in the chair as if getting comfortable. That look on her face told him that he couldn't easily get rid of her even if he wanted to, and she intended to stay until she was ready to leave. At least Everly hadn't changed. He and Paisley had no choice but to change.

He took a moment to take in Everly's full appearance. Her hair was somewhat disheveled; and she had a smudge on her temple, which would make sense since she'd gotten up close and personal when helping him out of the vehicle. At least she hadn't gotten burned like he had. She wore a dark blue windbreaker—she'd obviously replaced the one she'd used to save him—and a dark blouse to go with khaki slacks. She'd remained trim and fit, and there was something new about her that hadn't been there before. If he had to guess, he would say that she now had a law enforcement demeanor. But maybe he could simply ask and learn the truth.

However, she beat him to the questions. "So, what are you up to these days, Sawyer?"

"I was just about to ask you the same thing."

"Well, I asked first." She smiled. "I'll share my story after you share yours."

"Fair enough. My story is boring." Just the way he liked it. "I have my own import-export business, logistics management, that sort of thing."

"And what do you import or export?"

"I should clarify that I'm a consultant, and others hire me to assist them."

She lifted her chin. "Ah, I see. That sounds interesting."

He took that to mean she didn't understand at all. He thought he might have read in her eyes that she wanted to know what had happened to him after he disappeared— and that was the true reason behind her question. Maybe he would tell her one day, if the opportunity presented itself.

A few moments of silence passed as Everly waited for him to share more.

When he didn't, she continued, "But what about the rest of your story?"

"Maybe some other time. Now it's your turn." He glanced at his watch again before he realized he was being rude—but he was worried about Layla.

When he looked up, she hadn't missed him watching the time. "My brothers and I work together at Honor Protection Specialists."

He sat up taller at this news. "Protection specialists? As in, you're a bodyguard?"

"Well, it's a bit of both security and protection and some investigating. We have a lot of combined experience that lends itself to the whole shebang, if you will."

The whole shebang. That was a phrase he hadn't heard since his days with Everly—it was one she often said— and the memory warmed him.

Could it be? He smiled. "I think you might be the ab-solute perfect solution for a problem I have."

Arching her pretty brows, she sat forward. "And what would that be?"

"My niece, Layla, needs protection."

Her left brow arched even higher. "Your niece. Needs. Protection."

He got that she was struggling to believe what she heard. "Yes."

Everly leaned back and crossed her arms. "Well, then, I guess you'll need to tell me the rest of the story."

Indeed.

Everly reined in her surprise at his request to protect his niece, though she would admit to herself the news had stunned her.

"The rest of the story, as you called it, is…complicated. At this juncture, I'm not sure how much is relevant. What steps do I need to take to secure your employment?"

He'd suddenly shifted from a car-accident victim to determined and professional, and he had an edge about him that hadn't been there when she'd known him be-fore. He stared at her—his dark brown eyes penetrating, measuring her—as he waited for her answer. Everly drew in a breath and shifted her demeanor as well. She could certainly act in a professional manner, too, even though they'd known each other—well—before; so she thought that with a shared past, they were at least friends, loosely speaking. But…people changed.

"Um…well, usually, when we take on clients, we de-cide as a group. So you could request—"

"Please, Everly. For…old times' sake."

There it was. He was shifting again—friends now. *Old*

times' sake? She bit back her retort and pushed down her frustration.

Everly stared into the brown eyes that pleaded for her help. And she couldn't deny that she wanted to help him, with or without consent. "I just need to run it through Ayden at the very least. We work together, but he founded the company and is really in charge. And to do that, I'll need more information. The *what* and the *why*."

Now she would hear his story, she hoped. Unless protecting his niece had nothing at all to do with what happened to Sawyer and Paisley—and really, that had been years ago. Everly had no reason to think his request was connected.

"Are you saying you don't work for someone as a bodyguard just because they feel they need protection?"

"I'm saying that knowing why protection is needed helps us to know the full extent of the possible danger, which is another service we provide—threat analysis. If you think about it, knowing the risk is the only way to truly provide protection. From what does your niece require protection? Bullies at school or something more sinister?" She hoped for the former but sensed a darker reason behind his request.

He pursed his lips and stared at the wall behind her as if measuring how much he would tell her.

He might need a little nudge. "I won't do it if I don't know what's going on."

His eyes turned darker, almost black enough to match his hair. "Even to protect an innocent little girl?"

"That's not fair, Sawyer, and you know it. If you want her protected, then you'll tell me what's going on."

"That's just it. I can't be entirely sure. I think someone has been following me. I called a service for a bodyguard for her yesterday, and then today I saw my tail again."

"Wait. If you already have a service in place, why ask me?"

He grimaced, but then his eyes softened. "Layla isn't happy with the big bouncer guy—and, frankly, I'm not either. But you, Everly…" His cheeks dimpled with his smile. "Layla would adore you. Please do this. Me running into you again seems like an answer to my prayers, and I guess it's the silver lining in this whole Mack truck–car fire business."

She bit back her own smile. This guy knew how to pull on her heartstrings—and that was the old Sawyer she'd known before. She would say yes, definitely yes—even without the official go-ahead. But before she did, she would gain as much knowledge as she could.

"Any thoughts on why someone might want to follow you?"

"I wish I knew, but I'm concerned about Layla because… Because…" The way he stared into her eyes from a deep, broken place, it was like he was willing her to understand.

And Everly remembered. "I get it. You and Paisley were kidnapped."

He slowly nodded. "I won't let that happen to Layla."

How did she ask her next question delicately, without overstepping? "You were kidnapped before and ransomed because of your father's fortune. Is it that sort of situation that concerns you now?"

"No. I made sure of it. But I believe that if our father had acted sooner—because he suspected someone had been watching—we would not have been kidnapped."

"And someone has been watching you." He was on top of things, then. "So you've talked to the police."

"I gave my statement about the accident today."

"Did you share the details you just shared with me?"

"Not yet, but I will."

On top of things, except for this one important detail. And in that, Everly sensed he was hiding something, but she might need to earn his trust in a bigger way before he would tell her everything she wanted to know. And now that she thought about it, she wanted to know plenty. She wanted answers to those questions that had arisen after he and Paisley had disappeared. She couldn't help him, couldn't learn more, if she didn't work with him now.

Way to justify this, Everly.

"Listen." He stood and put his hands in his pockets. "I don't know what's going on now, but I won't risk Layla's life."

Layla's *life*? "Do you believe this could be a deadly threat, even though you claim you don't know why someone would follow you?"

"Believe me when I tell you, I *don't* know why. As to the deadly threat…" The intensity in his demeanor was answer enough, but he added, "I can't afford to take that risk."

An appropriate response. She admired him for stepping up.

"And what about *your* life, Sawyer?" After all, she'd seen that guy watching right before the wreck. Then after the wreck as well. Watching and waiting.

And she hadn't told the police about that, either, but she couldn't be sure, and bringing it up could draw attention to her complete paranoia about her own issues and her past.

"I'm hiring you to protect Layla. She's my priority. I can protect myself."

She stood, too, and suddenly the small space grew even smaller. Sawyer's charismatic presence could suck all the oxygen from a room.

And the fact that he affected her so strongly gave her

doubts about working with him. *What are you doing, Everly?* "Okay, I'll do it on one condition. If you want me to be effective, I need to be included in the investigation so I know what's going on." As for Ayden, Caine and Brett, if they hesitated, she would convince them the Honor Protection Specialists needed to partner with Sawyer to protect his niece.

The nurse opened the door and stepped into the room, bringing relief to the increasing tension. She provided Sawyer with his discharge instructions.

While she went over the paperwork with Sawyer, Everly stepped out into the hall and called Ayden. She waited for him to answer and thought back to what had happened between her and Sawyer long ago. Everything had changed the night that Sawyer and his sister, Paisley, had been kidnapped at nineteen. He hadn't been the same. She'd had to read all about it in the news because Sawyer had been focused on recovering and helping his sister—and they had both given up their inheritance, their shares in their father's conglomerate, Blackwood Holdings. An interesting reaction to being kidnapped and held for ransom because they had a wealthy father. All she could think was they didn't want to live with that fear in their future or for their children. Or had relinquishing their wealth been about something more? Something involving their father?

Everly could understand much of what they went through since her own father, Judge Pierson Honor, had allegedly been involved in accepting bribes, something she and her siblings had only recently learned. She shook her head at the awful truth. Her mother had been an FBI special agent. Both parents were gone now, and she didn't like to think even one negative thought. Believing something awful about parents you looked up to and believed in was brutal. At some point, Sawyer had walked away from his father.

At some point, a person needed something good to believe in.

Everly trusted and believed in God, and she hoped that was true for Sawyer.

When the call went to voice mail, Everly left Ayden a detailed message. She didn't think Sawyer had time to wait for their decision-making process—a vetting procedure that would protect them and their clients—and she would be there to protect Layla.

She waited in the hallway for him to exit and considered what he'd told her. Sawyer must have ideas on why someone had followed him, and she hoped to find those out too. Her next assignment wasn't scheduled to start for a couple of weeks. She wanted to take this on. After dealing with someone who had stalked her in the past, she'd taken classes in defensive moves, boxed at the local gym every week and graduated top of her class at the police academy, eventually working for the Tacoma PD until she transitioned to Honor Protection Specialists.

Everly was prepared to protect the niece of the man she used to love.

TWO

The nurse left him alone in the room to stare at the discharge papers. Everly had stepped into the hall, and now she wasn't looking at him with her lovely eyes, that intense gaze that could see right through him.

What was I thinking, asking her to protect Layla?

Sure, Layla would adore her, but that could be a problem. He and Everly had a history, and it was for the best to keep whatever he'd sensed between them today in the past.

He'd just have to see this through. He snatched up the papers and scraped a hand through his hair. Looked at his bruised face in the mirror and groaned. He looked as bad as his body felt. He left the room, half hoping that Everly would be gone, but she stood across the hall, waiting for him. Of course she would be, and a big part of him was also relieved.

Hiring her was the right decision. It was going to be okay. He could keep his distance from her, protect his heart—protect them both. Just because she was guarding Layla didn't mean his buried feelings for her needed to surface again. For all he knew, she had a significant other in her life by now. A boyfriend or husband. Why was he even thinking about any of this?

"I see you're still here," he said.

She shrugged and pushed away from the wall. "Why wouldn't I be? I'm going to protect Layla."

"Wait. Just like that? I thought you needed the green light."

"I'm here, Sawyer. Let's do this. With your car's condition, you'll need a ride. I'm happy to drive you."

"Don't I need to, um…sign documents?"

"Normally, yes. As soon as I get them, you can sign them digitally. I'm assuming you aren't concerned about the cost."

"No." He headed down the hallway with Everly in his wake. His muscles ached and his head hurt, but he couldn't afford to take pain relievers that might impair his reaction time. In any case, at least he wasn't driving.

Everly ushered him to her SUV, and he got in the passenger side. He waited for her to get into the driver's seat.

"I'll contact the other bodyguard service and let them know what's happened, and also give the bodyguard— Zach Brasher—a heads-up that you're taking his place." He blew out a breath. "It all feels like so much is happening."

Has happened.

Because it has! A familiar sensation washed over him—the same panic he'd felt when he and Paisley had been taken.

No, God, please. Don't let this happen.

Why did he sense evil pressing in on him from all sides?

The air seemed too thin, which couldn't be true. He reached up to loosen his collar, except his collar was already loose. He wasn't wearing a tie.

Everly turned to him. "Just take a deep breath."

She studied him, her eyes gently searching.

He let her presence, her reassurance calm him.

"It's going to be just fine," she said. "I have a good feeling about this."

With her in this with him, he did too. *A good feeling. And a bad feeling.* "I'm glad you're doing this. First things first, I need to introduce you to Layla. I'd prefer to do that at home and not out in public in case there's a scene."

Everly had started her vehicle, then steered out of the parking garage. "Oh, really? It's like that, is it?"

"She's twelve going on twenty. What do you expect? She needs a mother." Man, he wished he hadn't added that last part.

"Okay, where am I going?"

"Let's pick her up from school. I'll explain when we get home."

"What time does she get out of school?"

"Three thirty, but I want to get her now. Head to Ridgeway Middle School."

"That's on Blue Island." She shot him a surprised look.

"It's more laid-back." A hidden refuge in the chaos.

Everly said nothing more but followed the directions delivered by the female voice coming from the GPS navigator.

"Let's not talk too much in the car with Layla. At home, we can talk privately about how best to protect her."

"Knowing more about the threat is going to be essential."

She was fishing. *All in good time, Everly.* And yet he hoped he wouldn't have to share too much.

Leaning his head back against the seat, he rested and tried to ignore the pain, the constant throbbing. He needed to relax for a few minutes before picking up Layla. Introducing her to Everly would require a lot of mental and emotional energy. He never imagined a twelve-year-old could drain him so much. He loved her with all his being—but he could admit she was a drama queen.

Thank You, Lord, for bringing Everly into this.

"Sawyer, I hope you'll tell the police that you believe someone followed you. Your accident today could be something more."

"I'll tell them if it comes to that. I can't prove anything."

"I might have seen someone watching before the wreck."

He opened his eyes. Sat up. "Explain."

Everly told him she'd been suspicious of a guy in a nearby alley. He had seemed to be waiting or watching for something. Expectant.

"Yeah, well, that's nothing the police can really go on, is it?"

"Don't discount that they can help, okay? At the very least, we need to bring it up to them. They could review security footage in the area."

"I hired you to protect Layla—nothing more." The words came out brusque. Not what he'd intended.

Maybe bringing Everly into this had been a bad idea in that he didn't want to put one more person in danger; but on the other hand, he knew that she was the best person for this job. With Everly watching, the chances Layla would try to escape the intrusion of a bodyguard were far less.

"Understood."

Oh, now he just felt bad. "I'm sorry, Everly. We'll talk about it more later. Let's focus on getting Layla and explaining everything at the house."

"Yes, sir."

Great. He'd offended her. "I'm not at my best at the moment."

"That's understandable. Take it easy. I'm the one who needs to apologize for pressing you."

"You're fine."

Comfortable silence finally settled between them. One of his biggest regrets from years ago was leaving her behind. They could have had something special together, something lasting, but his life had blown up and obliterated his connections.

He struggled to comprehend, to believe that he was even here now, in this vehicle with her. He never could have imagined this scenario.

A second chance, Lord?

No. He didn't deserve it. Nor would he do that to Everly. His life was too filled with secrets, and he couldn't hurt her again.

Staring out the window at the lush green foliage of the Pacific Northwest, he made a mental list of everything he needed to do, including contacting the insurance company regarding his charred vehicle so he could get it replaced as soon as possible. But he couldn't help but think about Paisley.

After the kidnapping, they'd sold off their shares and given their inheritance to charities. Part of their goal had been to get out from under their father's thumb. Sawyer could see Layla already starting to act up in that regard. Though he was not her father, she opposed Sawyer at every turn as if he was anything like his now-deceased father had been.

Maybe he was but just couldn't realize it.

He released a slow exhale and with it, let go of his apprehension. "I'm sorry, Everly. I'll tell you what I can, just be patient with me."

"I shouldn't make demands. I know you've gone through

a lot. And caring for your niece? I hadn't realized that Paisley was gone. What…happened?"

"There's no easy way to say this. Paisley's husband was abusive. She left him when Layla was very young. But he kept coming after her. A restraining order didn't protect her, so she tried to disappear, but he found her and…killed her."

Everly swerved off the road and immediately stopped the vehicle. "Oh, Sawyer, I can't believe it." She turned to him.

And in the look of horror in her gaze, he recognized another look. A *knowing* look… Had Everly been stalked? Abused? She didn't voice the words, but he could hear them reverberating through his mind all the same.

Where were you, Sawyer, when Paisley needed you the most?

Everly couldn't help her reaction to the news. She'd had to stop the vehicle. Stop so she could catch her breath. No way could she focus on the road until she processed this news. "I'm so, so sorry. I didn't know. I hope I haven't overstepped by asking."

"You couldn't have known, and there's nothing wrong with asking."

Everly stared at her hands trembling on the steering wheel and shook her head. Sawyer and Layla needed help, more than Everly could give them, but she would be there for them in this one thing, no matter what her brothers decided. They'd known about her broken heart and could very well want to shut her down in this; but with this additional news, her protective barriers weakened, and she felt a deep affinity for Sawyer and the niece she hadn't yet met.

"And…Layla's father?"

"He was wanted for murder and tried to escape. He died in a fiery car crash."

A fitting end, but poor Layla. Poor Sawyer. Grief overwhelmed her. She lifted her face to his, but he stared ahead as if reliving another horrible addition to his past. "And if we don't want to die in a fiery crash, maybe you should pull back into traffic. I don't feel comfortable sitting on the shoulder with all those cars whizzing by."

"Oh. Sorry. You're right. I just…needed a moment."

"It's okay. I understand. Listen, you're probably wondering where I was during Paisley's crisis. I was working overseas. She didn't tell me. I don't know why she would have kept that from me other than she was embarrassed. She was stubborn and prideful, and she didn't want me to know that I'd been right about the jerk. She shouldn't have married him. I'm not going to blame her. I should never have moved halfway across the world from her. All we had was each other in terms of family. I should have stayed in the States. I should have been there for her."

"What were you doing earlier today, before the crash?" She thought she had an idea.

"Paisley is buried at the Evergreen Cemetery. She was laid to rest there four years ago today."

Sawyer was finally opening up and sharing.

"I had gone to place roses on Paisley's tombstone when I spotted the same Cadillac that had followed me last night."

"And I take it you didn't get a license plate number."

He put his elbow against the window and rubbed his forehead. "That's why today's accident could very well be on me. I had slowed down, hoping I wouldn't lose my tail."

"You wanted to get the number."

"Yes."

"Slowing through a green light had nothing to do with the truck that sped up."

"You thought that too?"

"Yes. Sawyer, I want to help you. To work with you and the police."

He remained silent at her suggestion. She pulled back into traffic, and the rain started coming down hard as she crossed the bridge over Puget Sound to Blue Island. She much preferred the bridge to the usual ferries, which took much longer.

"I know we still have a lot to talk about because I need to understand what's going on. You've told me that you don't know. But I'd like to add my investigative services here, even…unofficially."

He shifted in his seat as if that sounded more acceptable to him. What was that about?

"I don't intend to sit around and do nothing. I have no intention of waiting until someone else gets hurt. If you want to work with me…unofficially, I'll think about it."

"Okay, just tell me—is there a reason you don't want to work with the police?"

"Yes. It's called *privacy*."

Well, that was a new one. Or an old way of saying that he was hiding something, which she'd already figured out. But she couldn't know if hiding something meant anything illegal. People were allowed their secrets.

She parked at the school in the front.

"Since we're here early, I'll go in and get her," Sawyer said.

"Do you want me to go in with you?"

"No. Just wait here. The clock starts now. Look for anyone or anything suspicious."

She nodded and watched him head for the front of the building, then bound up the steps like he hadn't just rolled over in a vehicle and almost died in a fire. The man was…strong. Special. She didn't *want* to care for him like she used to. Couldn't afford to let her heart get tangled up in his life, because nothing had changed—he was still carrying the world on his shoulders.

In the rearview mirror, she spotted someone standing against a tree and watching. He could be waiting on a student, but something about him seemed out of place. He wore a dark rain jacket, with the hood pulled over his features. Could be something. Could be nothing.

But chills crawled over her arms.

Was she overreacting? Being paranoid?

Glancing around, she didn't see the blue Cadillac Sawyer mentioned had followed him. Everly got out of the vehicle and strode purposefully toward the man. As she approached, he pushed from the tree, then hurried down the sidewalk and cut across a heavily wooded park. She couldn't give chase because then she would be leaving her new clients.

But that was weird. His reaction to her approach could mean he was up to no good.

Everly returned to her car.

Sawyer exited the school with a less-than-happy Layla in tow. Everly remained outside the vehicle as Layla got in so she could inform Sawyer.

He joined her. Now was her chance to tell him without scaring Layla. "I think someone might have been watching over by the trees. I tried to approach but he rushed away as soon as he saw me. I didn't follow because I didn't want to leave you and Layla. You were right to hire someone to protect her."

He plowed his bandaged hand through his thick hair, then grimaced in pain. He stared at her hard, desperation in his gaze. "Thank you for agreeing to protect Layla, but Everly, that doesn't mean I want you to put yourself in danger. I'm glad you didn't go after him. Just stick close to Layla."

He leaned in closer. "At least at the house, with the security system I have in place, along with your presence, Layla will be doubly safe."

His gaze intense, his eyes skimmed over her face and her heart rate kicked up at his nearness.

Focus, Everly. Focus.

She could not get attached to this guy.

She thought back to the stalking incidents from the past that had forced her to become the woman she was today—able to face anything including working closely with the guy who'd once broken her heart.

THREE

Sawyer glanced around, but he didn't see the suspicious man. What Everly had shared about someone watching the school confirmed he'd made the right decision to hire a bodyguard. While he was glad he'd hired Everly to replace Zach, bringing her on included the challenge of not becoming emotionally involved with her again.

"You ready?" he asked.

She nodded. "Let's head home."

Home. The sound of the word coming from her left a strange feeling curling inside. "Good idea. You have your work cut out for you in winning Layla over, but if anyone can do it, I know it's you." He almost winked but caught himself.

They got back into the vehicle.

He thought Layla would have complained about taking so long, but when he glanced over his shoulder at the back seat, she was consumed with texting on her cell; it would seem she hadn't even noticed. Nor did she seem to care that they were in a different vehicle and a stranger was in the driver's seat. He shared a look with Everly, who merely smiled and started up the car. She entered the address that he gave for his home into the GPS and steered them away from the school.

They were halfway home before Layla finally spoke up. "Hey… Uncle Sawyer?"

He smiled to himself. *Now she notices.* "Yes, Layla."

"Whose car is this? Where are we going?"

"This is Everly Honor, an old friend, and it's her car. She's taking us home."

"What… What happened to your face? Your hand? Are you okay?"

He twisted around in the seat. "Yes, I'm fine. Thanks for asking."

Her cell phone was too much of a distraction since she was only just now noticing his injuries. After all, he'd walked her out of the school. "I'll explain more when we get home, but I was in a car accident today."

Layla gasped. "Oh, I'm so sorry." She leaned forward, pulling herself closer with the back of his seat. "Where did it happen? When? Did you go to the hospital? Oh, dumb question. Of course you did. Well, I'm glad you're okay. But please tell me what happened."

He almost chuckled at her barrage of questions. His head started to throb again, though. Leaning back against the seat, he sighed. "I'll tell you everything—just, please, let's wait until we get home."

Everly glanced at him, concern in her eyes. But she didn't ask him how he was. She already knew.

"I'd prefer to get it all out in one conversation," he said. "So, how was your day at school?"

"Fine. It's the same every day. Thanks for not making Zach pick me up today. That would be so embarrassing. Bad enough he was hanging around the house yesterday"

Sawyer smiled to himself. Layla was in for a big surprise, and he knew that her acceptance of Everly depended on the presentation.

Everly pulled up to the gated entrance of his house and

punched in the code he'd shared that opened the gate; then she drove up the long drive to the house. He wanted to tell her about the property and give her the grand tour, but that would have to wait until after he shared with Layla that Everly would be her new bodyguard. Was there a different term other than *bodyguard* that would be more appealing to Layla? He didn't know.

Everly parked in the front, leaving the garage empty. He exited the vehicle and led Everly and Layla to the front door. Once inside, Layla removed her backpack and headed to her room.

"Layla, I need to talk to you for a few minutes."

"Okay. I'm just putting my backpack away. I'll be right back."

She disappeared into her room. Sawyer inwardly groaned and glanced at Everly. She was checking out the house and had stopped to stare at the alarm system.

"I'll give you the security codes for that. Don't worry."

"After we get things squared with Layla, I'd appreciate learning everything there is to know about the property— for Layla's protection, of course."

Everly moved over to the refrigerator and opened it.

"What are you doing?" he asked.

"Do you keep snacks for Layla? I don't see much in here. Some yogurt, cheese, milk. Someone needs to go grocery shopping."

His head was starting to pound even harder. He hadn't hired her for the extra details. What was she doing? Still, she made a good point. "I'll make a list and get groceries."

"What's for dinner?" She arched a brow.

"We'll figure something out." He and Layla had been just fine for the last four years. Hadn't they?

"You're distracted, Sawyer."

"Okay. You got me. We eat takeout on most nights."

"I'm no cook, but maybe we should consider bringing it all home for the foreseeable future. I mean, considering the circumstances."

He blew out a breath as guilt pressed in on him—he'd really dropped the ball in caring for Layla, and he hated that someone else had to point that out to him. But if anyone was going to do it, he was glad it was Everly.

She was someone he could trust.

Eyes wide, Layla stepped into the kitchen and stared suspiciously at Everly, then looked to Sawyer. "What circumstances? What's going on?"

So the moment of truth was upon them.

Everly tried to soften her expression, push beyond her tenuous smile as Layla looked between her and Sawyer. The girl acted just like Sawyer had described—twelve going on twenty. She had long, straight soft brown hair and brown eyes. She would grow into a beauty just like her mother, Paisley.

Layla was waiting for an answer, and though Everly wanted to explain, she wouldn't take the reins from Sawyer. He would need to lead in this situation because, after all, he was her client and called the shots. Layla was his niece. He knew her better.

As the preteen stared them down, Everly recognized the flicker of fear in her eyes. Uncertainty.

"Well?" Layla asked again.

"That's what I wanted to talk to you about, honey."

Layla opened the refrigerator, reached to the very bottom and back of the fridge, and pulled out a soda. The last one.

Sawyer motioned to the kitchen table, where he and Layla sat, and Everly leaned against the counter to give them space. Maybe she should check the perimeter and give them even more space.

Nah. She wanted to hear this. Plus, she needed to answer questions. She hoped Layla wouldn't immediately put up a wall. Working with a client who didn't want you there made protective details that much harder.

Layla took a swig of her soda and tried to put on a nonchalant air.

"You weren't too thrilled with Zach," Sawyer said. "So I let him go."

Zach hadn't gotten much of a chance to prove himself, but Everly kept those words to herself.

"I don't know why I need a bodyguard. People will stare at me. While that's not a bad thing, I don't want to draw attention for the wrong reasons."

Sawyer arched both brows.

He shouldn't be so surprised that she would want attention. To Sawyer's credit, he didn't huff in frustration, but his features gentled. He clearly loved his niece and probably didn't want to scare her by telling her the full truth. But at some point, he might need to do just that.

Everly stifled her own huff. She'd love to hear the full truth as well.

Sawyer glanced at Everly. "As I mentioned earlier, Everly is an old friend. She's going to hang out with us for a while."

"Wait. So Zach isn't around because I didn't want a bodyguard. Now Everly is here to hang out. What does that mean? Is she hanging out because you two are dating?" She waggled her brows.

Everly wanted to step in and set the girl straight, but she held back.

Sawyer cleared his throat. "No. We're not dating. I hired

Everly today when I learned she works for a protection service."

"You mean, she's my new bodyguard."

Everly bit back the smile at Layla—she wouldn't be fooled by his tactics, and when Sawyer hesitated, Everly decided it was time to step in before Sawyer made a mess.

She moved over to the table and took a chair, then clasped her hands. "You could call me that, yes, but I prefer the term *personal-security detail*."

Layla studied her and took her time before she responded. "So…*you're* my security? I've never seen a woman bodyguard before."

"How many bodyguards have you actually seen, Layla?"

Layla's head bobbed up and down, and she smiled. "Fair point."

"I do much more than offer protection working with my brothers at Honor Protection Specialists." She glanced at Sawyer, hoping her words served as a reminder to him that she could offer more help than simply protecting Layla.

And him, by proximity.

Layla took another swig. "Maybe you can tell me why I need protection."

"Sure. Your uncle has his reasons for believing there's a potential threat to him and, by extension, to you, and he's not a man to sit idly by and let anything happen to you. Be very glad that he loves you and takes steps to protect you."

"I…I guess that makes sense." Layla suddenly smiled. "I hope you're more fun than Zach was. He had no sense of humor."

Everly chuckled. Layla obviously thought protection-detail services included babysitting—or rather, entertaining her too. Everly would do her best on both counts. "I hope I'm more fun too. I also think it would be best if we got groceries and hung out here for our meals, at least until the threat is over. So can you make me a list of what you like to eat? The both of you?"

Sawyer's eyes widened. "Really, Everly, that's not necessary. You're going above and beyond—"

"Think of it as part of my protective strategy, Sawyer. Let's stock up and stay in. Less trips out for food will make my job easier.'

She held his gaze and thought she saw admiration, and a flicker of something more. That *something more* she had to avoid at all costs. The man had crushed her heart before, and she wouldn't let that happen again.

Once groceries were bought at a nearby grocery store—at least what they could get from the list—Everly and Layla stocked them away while Sawyer returned a few phone calls. He stepped into the kitchen and watched them.

A funny look came over his face when Everly closed the last cabinet.

He crossed his arms. "Are you ready for the grand tour of the place?"

"Sure. Layla, you want to come?"

When the girl's demeanor shifted as if she would decline, Everly said, "I'd love for you to be the one to give me the tour. Your uncle can fill in any holes you leave."

Layla's eyes briefly widened with her smile. "Challenge accepted."

Everly hid her sigh of relief. She didn't plan on leaving Layla alone in the house and was grateful the girl seemed to be responding well to her presence. She felt Sawyer watching her, studying her, but she didn't look at him, because she might give away too much of what was going on inside to both him and Layla. The girl was sharp and didn't miss much, though she pretended to be oblivious when texting.

Everly wouldn't give Layla's secret away, though.

"Lead the way." Everly's 9 mm Glock was holstered at her waist.

"First, you should know Uncle Sawyer keeps cameras on the property, and you can view them in the security room." Layla moved down a short hallway off the kitchen and stood by the door. "But he keeps the room locked."

Arching a brow and smirking, Layla crossed her arms. *Oh, now I see how it is.* Layla would use this opportunity to point out what she believed were offenses.

Layla eyed Sawyer as he dug the key from his pocket. Seriously?

He unlocked the door, then fished out his cell. "I can view the security cameras on my phone too."

It wasn't Everly's place, but maybe Sawyer could offer Layla a little trust instead of locking her out. Still, he must have his reasons.

She joined Layla and Sawyer in the small room and looked at the monitors. "Does an alarm sound when the motion sensors trigger the cameras?"

"They're not turned on with motion sensors but are off-grid CCTV cameras. Motion sensors trigger an alarm when someone physically crosses onto the property."

"A perimeter alarm, then. What about deer? That must be a problem if you're using motion sensors."

"I have deterrents in the woods near the cameras—but yes, the occasional deer or raccoon can set the alarms off. It's only mildly annoying."

Layla showed Everly the rest of the house, and together they checked all the windows to make sure everything was locked up.

"At least the property is protected and you're aways

on alert." Everly smiled at Layla. She had to wonder why her uncle was so protective. What did she know?

"And if you're ready for the outside tour," he said, "I have an extra raincoat."

"That sounds like a plan. Let me get dinner in the oven before we head outside." They headed through the house, back to the kitchen.

"Is there anything I can do to help you?" Layla asked.

"Maybe." Everly needed to earn her trust. Then again, she was here to protect her, not become her BFF.

Before Sawyer closed the security door, Everly glanced at the cameras. Something flashed then was gone. What had she seen? She wished he would leave the door open, and she might talk to him about that. But later.

Layla received a text and headed down the hall to her room. So much for the help. This wasn't part of Everly's job, but Layla was safe in the house, and dinner would only take a few minutes. Everly refused to stand outside Layla's bedroom door like…well, the proverbial image of a bodyguard.

She pulled chicken breasts from the fridge, then set the package on the counter. Sawyer approached from behind.

She turned to face him and glanced at the packaging. "I'm going out to check the perimeter. Do you think you can marinate this with your one good hand?"

He groaned. "I can order delivery."

"Seriously, Sawyer. This isn't hard."

"I need the recipe."

She washed her hands, then set the fajita-seasoning packet on the counter.

"You're cheating?" he asked.

"I never said I was a chef."

He stepped closer and she gazed up into his dark eyes. She could smell his musky scent. His shoulders were broad, and the stubble on his jaw looked rough. What would it feel like to kiss that mouth?

Stop it.

"I didn't hire you to cook or guard the compound."

"I…I thought I saw something. I'm here to protect her, and I need to make sure the grounds are safe first."

He stepped closer, his brow furrowing. "You saw something? Then I'll go."

"I was with the Tacoma PD, Sawyer. I'm trained in defensive moves and… Let me do my job."

His frown deepened, and before he could protest, she grabbed the seasoning packet and thrust it against his chest. "And you can learn to do a better job here in the kitchen."

Once she escaped his nearness, she could think.

Telling him to cook meals for Layla isn't my job.

Nor was cooking them.

She tugged her jacket tight, pulled the hood over her head and then stepped outside. Gun in hand, she made her way around the house to check the perimeter, then headed into the woods surrounding the property. She would approach the area where she thought she'd seen something reflective.

They hadn't discussed the details of this arrangement and, in many situations, the protection detail only involved protecting the individual when escorting them outside of the home; but if Everly was needed to be involved 24/7, then one of her brothers could switch out with her. Though she honestly didn't think Sawyer would bring anyone else into the protection detail, and the threat level wasn't quite there yet—or was it? With the car accident, it certainly could be, but there was no definitive proof yet.

Dusk would fall soon, and she wanted to clear these

woods before nightfall. Sawyer's cameras didn't cover every inch of the area, so there were holes. He was banking on an intruder not knowing where he'd hidden cameras. The woods were so dense here, they were a pain to traverse. The rain trickled through the thick foliage—evergreens and too many kinds of trees to name, sword ferns and berry bushes. Finally, she found the spot she'd seen on-screen. She eyed the camera and then glanced down.

Trampled foliage. Someone *had* been here. But the motion sensors hadn't triggered an alarm or alerted them to an intruder. Maybe he'd been just out of range. She needed to find out more about how the security system worked out here.

She moved the bushes back and spotted the footprints, and then something else… A lens cap—to binoculars? She grabbed it with a glove and wrapped it up, stuck it in her pocket.

Suddenly, a strong arm hooked around her throat from behind.

FOUR

Sawyer was looking at the cameras the moment a man attacked Everly.

She was in trouble. Would she want his help? Or believe she could take care of herself? He didn't care what she thought. He wouldn't sit in this house and simply watch as someone attacked her. Grabbing his gun, he armed the house as he fled out the door, raced across the field to the woods. He shouldn't have let her go on her own—but then again, she had insisted she was trained to defend herself as well as apprehend bad guys.

Fighting the overgrown path to get to her, he shouted, hoping to distract her assailant.

There. He spotted them.

He rushed forward but jumped back when she freed herself from the man's grip with a headbutt, then whipped around and landed three punches to his gut like she was in a boxing ring. When the man turned to escape, she kicked him in the kidney. The attacker stumbled away and then picked up speed.

Everly pulled her weapon. "Freeze!"

But he continued forward, disappearing into the darkness.

Growling, Everly started after him, but Sawyer grabbed

her arm. She reflexively tried to land a punch, but he blocked it.

Her eyes widened. "I'm sorry!"

He backed off and held his hands up. "No need to apologize. It was the heat of the moment, the rushing adrenaline."

She nodded. "I was in defense mode. And now I need to go after him."

Everly started forward, but he stopped her again.

She yanked her arm free. "Let me go! I need to get him."

"Layla." He said the one word, the name. The reason he'd hired Everly.

She stopped in her tracks.

They could both run after this guy, but he doubted they would find him, especially on this cloudy, rainy night. Sawyer couldn't leave Everly to find the guy on her own, but neither could he leave Layla alone.

"Why did you leave her?" She sent him an accusing look.

He fisted his hands at his sides. "Someone was attacking you!"

"Someone say my name?" The young voice bounced against the trees that were dripping with rain.

And Layla stepped up behind Sawyer.

"What are you doing here?" he huffed out, failing to hide his frustration. "You should have stayed in the house."

She seemed oblivious to what happened around her most of the time, always on her cell, texting or scrolling through the latest, greatest social media app. Something. He hadn't stopped to think she might come looking for them. He'd only thought to save Everly. He needed to have a long talk with Layla and come up with the appropriate response to every situation.

"Let's go." Everly ushered Layla out of the woods, and they hiked toward the house, with Sawyer flanking them.

As if it hadn't already rained enough, the low-hanging clouds released a sudden, heavy load, drenching them.

After slowly crossing the field, Sawyer finally stepped back inside the house after the women and shut the door behind him.

He armed the house, noting that Layla hadn't set the alarm when she'd come to look for him. What happened tonight couldn't happen again.

They shed their rain jackets, water dripping all over the floor.

The smoke alarm blared.

Everly headed to the kitchen and looked back at him. "What did you do?"

"I put the chicken on to fry."

"No… I meant for you to marinate it." She rushed into the kitchen and found the smoking pan.

He grabbed a potholder and removed it, then turned on the stovetop fan and opened a window to air out the house. The window alarm beeped, and Sawyer turned it off.

Layla started laughing. Hard. *What in the world?*

She caught her breath. "You two are hilarious. I haven't had so much fun in a long time."

While he hadn't wanted to scare her, Layla obviously had no idea how serious the situation had just gotten. He glanced at Everly, who hadn't said a word, but he could see the wheels in that sharp brain of hers turning, moving at light speed.

"I'm going to clear the house to make sure no one came inside while we were all gone. Then we'll figure out dinner." Everly's expression said it all.

She now understood her protection detail services

wouldn't be so easily rendered under these circumstances. Layla wasn't the target here, but he would act as though she was in direct danger, thanks to her proximity to him. He wouldn't take the risk that his father had taken with his children. Though Sawyer wanted to shield Layla from knowing the worst of it, maybe it was time they had a heart-to-heart talk about the danger.

"I know you want to talk to her, so go," Layla said. Her eyes suddenly brightened. "And I know what we can have for dinner. It's simple and fast. I'm glad Everly suggested we get groceries and let me get all my favorites."

Way to win a teenage girl over, Everly.

He looked at her. She was growing up so fast, and telling her the truth about the danger wasn't what he wanted to do. The smoke alarm had finally stopped, and he shut and locked the window and reset the window alarm, then went in search of Everly.

He saw the attic ladder pulled down, and he climbed up to find Everly. "What are you doing up here?"

"I was clearing the house since Layla didn't set the alarm when she came out to find us. The attic was the last place I checked." She had turned on the light, and the one bulb hanging from the ceiling cast long shadows. "Let's go back down. We shouldn't leave Layla."

He climbed back down the ladder and held it for her— as if she needed his help—when she slipped down behind him. He put the ladder back up and closed the hatch, then turned around and found himself standing close to her, looking down into her eyes.

Her hair was still wet. "I'm sorry that she was left alone, Sawyer. Please know that I can take care of myself. You shouldn't have left her. But I know you hired me to protect her, so this is on me. We need to talk about best practices and strategies."

She said it all so matter-of-factly, he thought she would turn and walk away; but instead, she stared up at him, searching. Her eyes were big, beautiful and luminous. Sawyer wanted to touch her cheek. Rub a strand of her soft hair between his fingers.

Instead, he said, "You're cold, and you probably didn't bring a change of clothes, since I sprung this protection detail on you. I guess…it's probably time for you to go, and we'll see you again tomorrow morning."

"I'm staying."

"What? I never intended for you to watch Layla for twenty-four hours."

"I think you need more protection than you realize. Someone was out there watching you through binoculars."

Binoculars? Air whooshed out of him. "How do you know?"

She tugged a lens cap wrapped in a glove from out of her pocket. "I found this on the ground, with the footprints. The disturbed foliage. Then he grabbed me. I didn't catch his face because of the mask. I suspect he knows you have a good security system and cameras, so we won't catch him without a face covering." She drew in a breath as if to speak, then hesitated.

"What else?"

"I think the guy in your woods could be the same guy who was watching from the alley just before the wreck. I can't be sure, but he seems to have the same build. The guy watching at school is smaller so it wasn't him."

And she'd sent the bigger man running. Amazing. Admiration for her swelled up inside. He hadn't truly known her skill level when he'd hired her, his only thought being that she would be the best fit for Layla. Before he could stop himself, he lifted his good hand and wiped the rain droplets from her cheek. The touch sent a charge up his arm, and her pupils widened.

Yes, he was still attracted to her—in every way possible. All the more reason why he should keep his distance. He took a step back and broke the connection. "I'll grab a blanket, start a fire so you can warm up, and we'll talk about what's next."

"Dinner's ready," Layla called.

Everly smiled. "Sounds like food is what's next."

He watched Everly walk away and head down the hall toward the kitchen. She was back in his life to protect Layla—but unfortunately, she'd brought a danger of her own to him, personally. To his heart.

Everly left Sawyer standing there. She needed to put distance between them, and fast. The man's touch had affected her more than she could have imagined, especially coupled with the spark of longing in his dark eyes. She couldn't allow herself to grow emotionally attached to him; it would cloud her judgment in the middle of this assignment.

But that wasn't the only reason.

Sawyer had broken her heart before, and given that he still had secrets, she wasn't about to fall for the guy only to have him break her heart all over again. She was older, wiser and stronger now.

In the kitchen, she saw the table fully set, and she smiled. "It looks great, Layla!"

"I hope you like chicken nuggets. I'm glad we got something that we could heat up in the microwave—otherwise we'd all be starving by the time we got something to eat."

Layla had dumped a prepackaged salad into a large bowl to go with the salad tongs and dressing. Easy enough.

Maybe after this was over, Everly could give her a few cooking lessons. *Wait.* She shouldn't be making plans to hang around this family after this was over.

But for now, she would smile and be grateful, and then check the perimeter again.

In fact, she didn't want to be rude, but she hoped their dinner would be over soon. They weren't supposed to be a big happy family here; but at the same time, she understood that if she wanted to effectively guard the pre-teen, she had to both earn her trust and learn to trust her.

Maybe Sawyer needed to beef up his domestic skills, but at least he'd practically perfected the sit-down family dinner. Layla completely focused on conversation with him, putting her cell phone aside—amazing. She listened to them talk about mundane and safe topics.

"Thanks for the great chicken nuggets, Layla," Everly said.

"And for salvaging the mess I made." Sawyer grabbed their plates as he stood. "I'll clean up."

"How about we talk about the elephant in the room before you do the dishes?" Layla stared her uncle down. "You haven't told me everything about why I need a bodyguard. You can start with telling me what happened in the woods tonight."

Everly gave Sawyer a look, encouraging him to address the issues and explain the elephant, as she took the plates from him. "You talk to her, and *I'll* do the dishes." Besides, it wasn't her place to explain. She preferred that Sawyer take care of it, or Layla would probably ask Everly too many questions, and she wasn't exactly sure which ones she could answer—especially since she didn't know all the answers.

"Someone has been following me. The first time I noticed it, I hired a bodyguard."

"Following you? That sounds scary. Who would want to follow you?"

"I don't know."

"What does that have to do with tonight?"

"Someone was in the woods, watching the house, and Everly confronted them and sent them running. I don't know who. I don't know why." He moved over to sit in the chair closest to Layla at the table and gripped her hand. "But I need you to trust me. Please be cautious and stick close to Everly until we have this situation under control. Do we have a deal?"

Everly glanced over in time to catch Layla's tenuous smile. "Okay. I guess so. But as soon as you know something, I want answers." She pushed away from the table and stood. "I'm going to my room. I have some homework to catch up on before bed." Layla looked over at Everly, who remained at the sink. "Is…is Everly going to take me to school and pick me up? I mean… I didn't like the idea of the other bodyguard chauffeuring me because it would be obvious what he was doing, but Everly is more like a friend. That is, if she'll switch out of that shirt with the HPS emblem."

Sawyer looked at Everly and, smiling, held her gaze. Her heart warmed. It seemed to confirm to her that Layla had accepted her.

"I think that can be arranged," Everly said. But those were the exact logistics she needed to work out with Sawyer.

After the dishes were done, she checked the perimeter of the house. When she was done, she found Sawyer pacing in the dimly lit living area, a fire burning in the fireplace. The romantic ambiance hit her. That couldn't have been his intention, and it frustrated her that her first thought went to romance. But she pushed it aside, ignored it—she had a job to do. She and Sawyer weren't a couple.

"We need to talk logistics, Sawyer." She kept her voice soft so Layla couldn't hear, in case she was trying to listen in. "But first, let's get your cameras set up on my phone too."

"I was going to suggest that."

After a few minutes of downloading the appropriate app and inserting the right codes, she was all set to view the various security cameras and alerts. "You have a good security system in place, but as you can see with what happened tonight, someone can still get through." Or even block the signals with the right software, depending on how determined they were to get at Sawyer.

"And you put this security in place even *before* someone followed you."

She studied him, hoping he would provide an explanation without her pressing. But when he said nothing, she continued, "I need to check in with my brothers, and if you want 24/7 protection—which I highly recommend under the circumstances—then I can arrange to trade out with them."

"No." He started pacing the small living room again.

"Are you saying that you don't want 24/7 protection?"

"I'm saying that you and I are enough. I don't want anyone else involved."

"Sawyer, my company is an extension of me. You have all our resources available to you."

"I want to keep this close and limit those who know about it."

"For reasons you won't share with me."

"Please, just trust me on this."

"Fine. But full disclosure, I am going to call in what happened tonight so there is at least a police report." She waited for his objection, but he merely nodded. "I'll at least need a few things. I can have one of my brothers bring the duffel that I keep at our headquarters."

He suddenly looked up, gratitude in his expression. "Thank you, Everly. You've been an answer to prayer for Layla."

He took a step forward, and her throat tightened as she remembered earlier in the hallway, when he'd touched her cheek. Was she making a mistake to agree to work with him? Then again, Everly didn't want to leave him and Layla without protection for even one moment. She could set aside her personal feelings about the man standing before her. Never mind his incredibly attractive face, athletic physique and good heart.

Never mind he was hiding something.

FIVE

The next morning, Sawyer planned to follow Everly as she took Layla to school.

With Everly's news that she'd suspected someone of watching from the alley as if anticipating the collision, it seemed to confirm that the crash had been engineered. He couldn't prove it, but he needed to get to the bottom of it so he and Everly had made their plans for the day. She would protect Layla, even while she was at school, and he would look into the accident.

And to do that, he first needed to speak with the man behind the wheel of the Mack truck. He'd sent his insurance company the police case number he'd been given and was told they would follow up with the trucking company. He hadn't been provided details on the driver. He'd been carted off in an ambulance, so it wasn't like he was there to ask the guy for his license. He hadn't been able to get the official report because the officer said it would take a few weeks to complete and wasn't yet available.

He looked at images of the accident posted online. All of the still shots and footage were of his vehicle burning. However, he found one shot of the truck that hit him—the driver was still inside. But he couldn't tell much about the man. Did he appear shocked or injured? Elated? Or satisfied?

And of course, no one caught the image of the man Everly claimed had been watching and waiting.

Waiting to finish me off if the car wreck didn't kill me?

He needed to get Layla moving so she wouldn't be late to school. "I'll wait outside."

"I'll set the alarms on the way out." Everly was preoccupied with something on her phone. "You don't need to wait. I've got this. Layla's coming."

"I'm following you in."

He left her to it and headed outside into a chilly, wet morning, and he waited by his vehicle. He'd removed the bandage over his burnt hand, which looked much better. It needed air instead of a bandage, in his less-than-medical opinion. He didn't have time to waste on small injuries. Still, his hand throbbed.

He'd just have to focus on something else, and he lifted his gaze to the beautiful five-acre property he'd secured a few years ago. He never grew tired of the sight of lush evergreens, spruce and cedars; the mountains in the distance that would soon be snowcapped; the salty scent of the ocean coming off Puget Sound.

Covering a yawn, he admitted to himself—for now—that Everly might be right about needing an extra person. He couldn't function for too long on little sleep, but he had every intention of finding out who was behind the danger and ending this soon.

Everly had already cleared the perimeter and even checked the vehicles for possible bombs, which she had whispered to inform him. He hadn't even considered that possibility, and the thought caused his pulse to spike.

Am I in over my head?

The door opened and Layla meandered to Everly's vehicle, but Everly made a beeline for him.

"Don't worry about Layla. I've got her. In the meantime, I sent you something that could help. Check your email."

"What did you send?"

"The preliminary police report for the accident. It includes the information on the truck driver." With those words, she pivoted and strode over to her vehicle, leaving him to watch her go.

And yeah, his mouth kind of hung open. Without the police report, he hadn't been entirely sure where to start, but Everly had gotten him something to work with. He might have spent the entire morning going in circles.

Before she climbed in, she glanced over at him and smiled. He suspected she'd meant to reassure him, but warmth started up in his belly at her simple gesture and amazing smile. She truly cared about her clients.

A knot formed in his throat. Deep down, he hoped she cared about him more than the rest of her clients.

For what reason or purpose? He was being ridiculous.

But the feelings rose, despite the fact that he tried to ignore them.

He didn't have time to check his email if he was going to follow her. She was already backing out, so he hopped into the rental Toyota RAV4 that had been delivered early that morning.

Sawyer followed Everly all the way to the school, where she pulled in behind the other parents dropping off their kids. *Other parents.* He watched Layla lean in and wave goodbye to Everly and then turn and bound up the steps and through the doors, happy-go-lucky—as if her life hadn't been turned upside down all over again.

A pang shot through his heart.

Sawyer shook off the melancholy. He took the bridge that connected Blue Island across Puget Sound to Tacoma. He stopped at a gas station to fill up and get the information he needed off the preliminary report. He opened up the email and found the details regarding the truck that had hit him. The officer believed the incident had been an accident, and the truck driver had been issued a ticket. No one had been charged with attempted murder.

What had he expected?

Sawyer's stomach soured. He wasn't so sure, and while he knew he could be acting paranoid, he would rather find out the truth than take the risk that the driver had intended to run him into the ditch.

Only thing…the report included the driver's name, Kevin Ellis, but for some reason not his personal contact information since the trucking company covered him. Maybe the completed report would include the information, but he didn't need to wait. Everly's email included that information—she'd gone that far with it. How was she able to find out so much so quickly? She'd mentioned HPS had resources and connections. That must be the reason.

Maybe he should take her up on her offer to assist in the investigation unofficially; it looked like she was already doing just that anyway.

He steered toward the industrial area where the trucking company was headquartered. Ellis might not be at work today, but Sawyer would start there.

While it was hard to believe the driver had intentionally rammed into him, he could imagine someone coercing him, blackmailing him or paying him off. And if the accident had been engineered and there had actually been a man waiting to finish him off, then Everly's sudden appearance on the scene—her rescue attempt, along with the bystanders catching footage on their cell phones, all of it—had likely saved Sawyer's life by scaring his intended killer away.

On the other hand, things could have gone a very different way yesterday. Everly could have been hurt because she'd tried to save him.

Still, despite her small size, she was tough and intimidating. She was athletic, fit and brave, and she carried a gun. He could keep going. She was different from the young woman in her late teens whom he'd known and had hoped to one day spend the rest of his days with.

Life had a way of changing people.

Sometimes for better.

Sometimes for worse.

One thing that hadn't changed was the effect Everly had on him. He thought back to that moment he'd touched her cheek and the raw sensations that had rushed through him, gripping him. He'd come very close to kissing her.

What was I thinking?

He was on double duty here. He had to protect them both from getting hurt again—by each other.

His life was too dangerous. Too secretive.

Could he really afford adding another person into his circle? Emotionally speaking, that is. Seriously. If it wasn't for Layla's reaction, he would have stayed with the original bodyguard.

At the trucking company, he found the main entrance and asked about Kevin Ellis, but the receptionist wasn't allowed to give out employee information. Sawyer asked to speak with the supervisor. Natalie Foster answered his request, and Sawyer explained to her that Ellis had been driving the truck that rammed into him and nearly killed him.

Ms. Foster put on a determined, strong front, but Sawyer recognized the fear in her eyes. "As you've already been informed, we cannot give out employee information. I'll have our lawyer give you a call."

Ah. She was concerned he planned to sue the company. "No, please. I just want to talk to him."

Ms. Foster hesitated, then said, "Walk with me."

She escorted him out of the building and into the parking lot. "Now, if you'll excuse me, I need to get back to work."

What? Well, that was just great. Sawyer had accomplished nothing. Ms. Foster turned to walk away but then paused. She twisted around to look at him. "You might as well know that Ellis doesn't work for us anymore."

"You fired him for an accident?"

"He quit. Cleared his stuff out last night."

"Was that so hard to tell me?"

"It's not information we're supposed to give, but you seem like a persistent man. I'm saving us both time." She nodded, then headed back into the building.

Sawyer absorbed that information. *Well, then, time to head to the guy's house.*

If Ellis had been coerced into purposefully ramming into him, how would he get him to talk when even the police had ruled it an accident?

Half an hour later, Sawyer sat a few hundred yards down from the man's house. He saw no vehicle. No movement. No life. Kevin Ellis had quit his job, and it appeared he'd left home for a while.

When finally Sawyer knocked on the door, no one answered. Then he spotted a neighbor just exiting his vehicle in the driveway. Sawyer hopped off the porch and strode over toward the neighbor's house.

"Hey, friend. I'm looking for Kevin. You seen him?"

The man gave Sawyer a wary look as he approached and stuck his hand out with a smile.

"Sawyer Blackwood. I'm an old friend and thought to stop by and surprise him. Just tell him when you see him that Sawyer was here."

The man quirked a smile. Good. He'd disarmed him.

"I might not see him for a while. He tossed luggage in his utility vehicle and headed out last night."

Sawyer wasn't surprised but let his disappointment show. "Too bad I missed him. Did he say when he'd be back?"

"Nah. Looked like he was in a hurry."

Great. Just great. The guy had skipped town—and that alone told him something.

Everly waited in her vehicle outside the school. She waited and watched. At times, when the drizzling rain let up, she got out of the car and walked near the school. The resources officer—a commissioned law enforcement officer—had been informed that she was there for Layla so she wouldn't raise any suspicions. If anything, her presence added another layer of protection. Sad that security was even required at schools.

The last bell of the day rang, and students began pouring through the doors. Everly had secured a special parking spot near the front exit, and she casually leaned against the car and waited for Layla. She exited the building, chatting with friends as she came down the steps with barely a glance at Everly. But obviously, she'd spotted the vehicle because she stopped walking and told her friends goodbye. They acknowledged her, then continued in conversation as they headed toward their own rides, and Layla hopped into Everly's vehicle.

Everly started up the car again.

Should I ask Layla about her day?

Or was that getting too personal? Kids were often annoyed by their parents' questions; then again, they were hurt if their parents didn't ask. Still, Everly wasn't her parent. She wasn't her mom. She didn't even rank as a friend.

As Everly approached the stoplight and maneuvered into the right lane to turn, Layla spoke up. "Would you mind if we went to the mall first? I'm working on a project at school, and I need supplies."

Everly turned into a drugstore parking lot and considered the request. "Layla, you know we bought groceries so we could stay home as much as possible until we know it's safe."

"Come on, please. Uncle Sawyer has kept me in a cage. I need to get out. Besides, my project is due in a few days."

"What's the project? Maybe I can help."

"It's fiber art. Most of what I need is at school, but I wanted to make mine special."

Her big brown eyes tugged at Everly's heart strings.

"I think I should talk to Sawyer about it first."

Layla sighed heavily for added drama.

Before Everly could text Sawyer, she received a message from him. Of course he would want to check in since this was Everly's first day.

How is Layla?

She smiled and replied.

She's safe and secure and wants to go to the mall for art supplies for a school project. I don't think it's a good idea, but I told her I would ask you.

Yes.

She replied to his text: Are you sure?

I trust you to protect her. Just make it quick.

See you in an hour.

She sagged and blew out a breath. Maybe she shouldn't have asked, but then again, she knew it was important for Layla's life to be as normal as possible. One quick trip for art supplies should be okay. The plan was never to keep her in a prison—or a cage, like Layla had said.

She shot Layla a tenuous grin, then put her cell away. "We're good to go, but we need to get in and out quickly, okay?"

Layla rewarded her with a genuine smile. Everly steered across the road. She headed toward the bridge that would connect them to the sprawling metropolis of Tacoma and Seattle. As always, Everly continued to watch the road. No one suspicious had appeared near the school today. While she appreciated that fact, she continued to think about Sawyer and if he was being followed. If someone would try to kill him again.

Be safe out there.

She'd wanted to ask him about his day and if he'd had any success finding out more about Kevin Ellis, but not while Layla was looking on. Besides, her focus needed to remain on Layla.

The bridge was half a mile out. Everly wasn't sure she completely bought Layla's claim she needed supplies. Maybe she could get her to share more. "Besides the art supplies, what else did you want to get at the mall?"

Maybe she could get the girl to talk about a boy she

liked, potential boyfriends or even secret boyfriends. All of it was good to know, and one might not consider it important in the protection scheme of things, but every detail mattered. Sawyer maintained that Layla didn't have a boyfriend.

Maybe not.

But chances were, the girl wanted one.

Layla giggled—an expected response. "Well, I also wanted to look at makeup. I mean, if we have time."

"Makeup?" Layla didn't wear any. Yet.

"When I asked my uncle the last time, he said I was too young."

"And when was the last time you asked?"

"Last week."

Oh, boy. Sounded like Layla was going to try to use Everly's presence to manipulate her uncle. Before she said more, she'd have to think on that one.

Crossing the bridge, Everly glanced in the mirror. Her vehicle was pressed in at the back and on the side, into a "wolf pack"—not a position she wanted to be in. Pressing the accelerator, she increased speed over the bridge's limit to move out of the pack. The white Tahoe in the left lane that she'd left behind increased speed too.

Not a good sign. Could be nothing, but Everly's heart pounded. The driver sped up and kept pace with her.

Everly's pulse soared. Time to take charge.

"Um… Everly?" Layla's voice shook.

"Hold on."

Preparing for what might come next, Everly tightened her grip on the steering wheel.

Lord, let me be wrong!

The Tahoe slammed into her vehicle from the side. Layla screamed.

Oh, no, you don't!

Determination surged as she gritted her teeth and veered to the left, avoiding the guardrail. The driver intended to force her vehicle through that guardrail and into the water below.

Layla started hyperventilating. "What are we going to do?"

Everly had to focus on getting them out of this, and then she could assist Layla. Fury boiled through her veins. Cars around them honked, and in the rearview mirror, she spotted a police cruiser's flashing lights. They neared the end of the bridge. The vehicle rammed her hard and wouldn't let up.

He really is trying to kill us!

Layla got on her cell. "I'm calling 911."

"Good idea, but I think the police already know." *And still this guy isn't letting up.*

The guardrail pressed into her vehicle, grinding against the metal on Layla's side. Layla dropped her cell and stiffened as she screamed louder.

"Everly…do something!"

Lord, what more can I do?

The guardrail ended with the bridge and space opened for her to make a move. She accelerated and forced her SUV through the opening. The other driver sped forward and clipped her left-rear fender…but his move backfired. His vehicle swerved and then flipped off the highway.

The breath whooshed from Everly as she pulled over to the shoulder and onto the grass to put more space between them and the road.

"What are you doing?" Layla still sounded terrified.

"I need to go on the offense here."

"What does that even mean?"

"It means you stay in the car and lock the doors. Call 911 and ask for an ambulance." The police cruiser that would soon catch up to them probably had already done so, but calling again hurt nothing and would give Layla something to do.

Brandishing her gun and chambering a round, Everly got out and crept toward the flipped vehicle.

The driver might be hurt, or he could be dead. But she couldn't let him slip away and try to kill them again on another day. Everly crept forward and slipped around, peering into the cab of the overturned vehicle. Empty.

Gone. He was just…gone.

Everly tucked her gun away and brandished her Honor Protection Specialists credentials as two police officers approached her, their guns raised and pointed at her. She lifted her hands along with the credentials. "I'm protective detail for my client. The driver of this vehicle tried to run us off the road. He tried to kill us."

One officer stayed with her and took her statement while others who had joined them surrounded the car. What would Sawyer think now that the police would be involved in searching for an obvious attempt on their lives? Though he wouldn't be happy, he would be relieved that Layla was okay. She glanced at Layla, who was watching from inside the car. Emergency vehicles— an ambulance and fire truck—arrived, along with a tow truck.

The officer with her was on his radio and cell, issuing orders back and forth. This collision of sorts had created a traffic nightmare. Everly stood off to the side while the tow truck got in position, and she answered more questions. She hated how her voice shook, and she tucked her trembling hands beneath her crossed arms. What was the matter with her? She'd better get her act together, or she would be in no condition to drive Layla to the mall.

The mall? No. Actually, they should head home as soon as the police were done with them.

"We'll locate the driver, Ms. Honor, and let you know. We'll contact you if we have more questions," the officer said.

Everly nodded and thanked the officers. She had a feeling they would definitely have more questions.

Everly had her own set of questions: Who had tried to run her off the road? Why exactly had they targeted Sawyer and, now, obviously, Layla too.

But it couldn't be helped—and maybe now, Sawyer would be willing to invite the police into this investigation.

Guilt filled her as she hiked up the hill toward the vehicle she'd left running on the side of the road, with Layla inside. Not a good safe place. As she approached, she could see the girl's tears. She'd been hired to protect her, and now she wasn't so sure that what had happened today wasn't on her. Sawyer might fire her.

A man was running, weaving his way through the police and emergency vehicles, heading straight for Everly's car.

Sawyer.

Layla jumped out and into his arms.

Everly had no illusions that Sawyer would give her the same treatment.

SIX

Sawyer squeezed Layla to him.

I could have lost you.

Layla tried to pull back, but he squeezed harder.

"Uncle Sawyer, let me go." Only then could he release her, but not all the way. He gently gripped her arms. "Are you okay? What happened? Where's Everly?"

"I'm right here." She stood a few paces away, feet spread wide and hands on her hips.

She put on an intimidating front, but he couldn't miss the fear swimming in her eyes.

He'd better release Layla before he gripped too hard and hurt her, but his heart beat at a painful pace.

"Uncle Sawyer, we're safe. We're okay. Take a breath before you have a heart attack."

A heart attack?

"What exactly happened?" He sounded breathless. Yeah, maybe Layla was right. "I was coming back from Tacoma and spotted the police cars, emergency vehicles. Then I saw your car with Layla inside. I..." He had to stop speaking to keep the shaking out of his voice.

"Everly saved us." Layla wiped at the tears on her cheeks and smiled.

Layla was so strong, and he was proud of her. Had he brought this on her?

"We can talk at home," Everly said. "I'll explain everything there—but right now, standing here out in the open probably isn't a good idea."

Or a safe place. "Right. You're right." He looked at Layla. "You can ride with me."

"No. I'm good. Everly knows what's she's doing." Before he could protest, Layla got back into the car.

Everly pursed her lips, sent him an apologetic look and shrugged as she made her way around to the other side of her vehicle. "We're headed right home. See you there."

As it turned out, he couldn't follow them because he'd parked pretty far away and had to get to there on foot.

"Uncle Sawyer, we'll give you a ride to your car." Layla had lowered her window.

He looked at the tangle of traffic thanks to the accident and shook his head. "No. I'll meet you there."

Sawyer watched Everly pull into traffic and head back toward the island as he made his way to the RAV4. He climbed in and hung his head. Let the adrenaline crash and his heart calm.

He suspected whatever had happened with the flipped vehicle had everything to do with someone trying to get to him. Still, first things first.

Sawyer needed to get home and find out exactly what had happened.

He maneuvered back onto the road and into traffic. Spotting the vehicle being loaded onto the tow truck, he got the license plate. This wasn't the Cadillac he'd seen following him. But he wouldn't take any relief from that.

He sped through traffic, steered onto the two-lane road out into the country on Blue Island and finally parked next to Everly's car in front of his house. Sawyer took a moment to calm his nerves before facing the two people who meant the most to him in this world.

The thought brought on a chuckle. He had to admit that he cared deeply for Everly—about her and her future. He always had. For some reason he couldn't fathom, God had brought her back into his life. He needed to remember that after this assignment, she would be out of his life once again.

As it should be.

If only the thought didn't unsettle him.

He hopped out of the RAV4 and hurried to the door, where Layla stood, holding it open for him. Though her eyes remained somewhat red from crying earlier, she smiled.

He hugged her lightly as he moved inside, then closed the door and set the alarm.

Everly emerged from the kitchen, holding out a mug. "Coffee?"

He took the cup, but at her gesture, a hundred thoughts exploded in his brain. Next she would ask him to sit down. He would do it before she asked. Sawyer headed to the kitchen and took a seat at the table, expecting Layla and Everly to follow. Setting the cup on the table, he left his still-shaking hands in his lap.

"One of you had better tell me what happened, and soon."

Everly took the seat across from him. "Someone tried to force us off the bridge."

"And Everly… Well, she was great." Layla grabbed a soda from the fridge, then sat down too. Apparently she'd recovered already. She popped the top, and the fizzing sound filled the silence.

"I got his license plate number."

"I did too," Everly said. "The vehicle belongs to an A. H. Holdings. I hope you don't mind that I asked for help in looking into who was driving."

He dipped his chin and stared at the table. "I need the help."

Layla received a text, and she hopped right up. "I'm going to my room, if that's okay."

"Wait." Sawyer took her hand. "Are you sure you're okay?"

"Yes. I'll be fine. I've got *you,* and… I have Everly now."

He absorbed her words; did she really mean them? "Let me know if you need to talk. Oh, and, Layla—we need to stick together for a while."

She huffed. "It's not like I go anywhere anyway, lately."

Then she trotted down the hallway, staring at her cell. Sawyer lifted his gaze and took in Everly's expression. "Well? I know you're holding back. You can speak freely now."

Everly moved from the chair to sit closer to him, he presumed so she could whisper. His heart pounded at the thought that she had something more, something worse to add to this situation. Or was it simply pounding at her nearness?

She took her time, appearing to take in his face. *What are you thinking?*

"I won't lie or sugarcoat things. For a hot minute there, the car trying to force us off the bridge terrified us."

Wanting to reassure her, he pressed his hand over hers on the table. He should have expected the surge, the spark of electricity that lit through him. But he kept his hand in place. "Thank you for your quick actions that saved my niece."

A soft smile edged into her lips. "Of course, Sawyer. You hired me to protect her, but I would have done it regardless. I hope you know that."

"I do."

She stood and squeezed his shoulder as she grabbed his mug.

"What are you doing?"

"The coffee's cold now. Do you want me to warm it up?"

"I didn't hire you to cater to my needs." He stood and followed her to counter.

She dumped the contents into the sink then turned to face him. "Take the rest of the day to get your head straight. We need time to regroup and come up with a plan on how to find out who is coming after you. This time they targeted Layla. You were right to make sure that she knows to stick close. She wanted to get out and about and—" Everly suddenly averted her gaze and breathed through her nose. "I had given my statement and answered more questions when you showed up. I'm sorry... I didn't get a chance to inform you sooner."

He stepped closer. "It's okay, Everly. Your quick-thinking and actions saved Layla's life. I made the right decision when I hired you. I'm glad you're here for her and...for me." The words warmed inside him, thudded around in his heart and landed in a soft place.

They meant much more than he'd intended.

His gaze dropped to her lips—of all places.

What am I doing?

She definitely should not be gravitating toward Sawyer. His presence drew her in, and she fought to control her need to be close to him. In his arms. She couldn't help herself... The tension between them pulled her forward as if against her own will. Her heart trumped her brain. Her breaths came quicker as she responded to his silent invitation to kiss.

Mere millimeters from his face, his lips, she held herself, hovering there. Wanting the kiss. Needing his touch. He held back as if he, too, was weighing the consequences.

A perimeter alarm dinged on both their cells.

The sound jarred through her.

Instantly, the world rushed in and broke the connection. Lifting her shoulders, she stepped back. He caught her gaze and held it as if wanting her to understand what he couldn't speak. Regret swam in his eyes—was that regret that he'd almost kissed her?

Another emotion surged through her. Pain. And memories of him breaking her heart.

Everly used all her energy to restrain her reaction.

They both tugged out their cells and reached for their guns.

The image on the security app revealed a man.

"I don't know him," Sawyer said.

"It's Detective Lincoln Mann." Everly knew Lincoln well and had worked with him while on the Tacoma PD. He was a friend to her brothers, too, and worked with Honor Protection Specialists services. Connections in law enforcement often paved the way to solving an investigation sooner.

Still, apprehension crawled over her skin. Sawyer might think she'd interfered with the process and was trying to pressure him to bring the police in. With the way he was staring at her, she suspected that was exactly what he thought.

The doorbell rang.

"What is he doing here?" He maintained an accusing stare as he made his way to the door, waiting for her answer.

Everly didn't like the biting look he gave her. "To investigate what happened today, I assume. What else?"

"Did you call him?"

She placed her hands on her hips. "No."

Hesitating, Sawyer stood near the door.

"Aren't you going to answer it?"

His scowl deepened, but then he seemed to force his face to relax and opened the door. "Can I help you?"

"I'm Detective Lincoln Mann. I was given this address by one of the officers on the scene of an accident involving your niece today. Apparently, Everly Honor is working for you."

"That's correct."

Lincoln glanced behind Sawyer to see Everly. "I have a few questions about the incident today."

Sawyer didn't move.

"Do you mind if I come inside?" Lincoln asked.

In answer, Sawyer opened the door wide and gestured for Detective Mann to enter. Everly knew that he wasn't happy that the police were now obviously getting involved, but just how long did he think he could keep this private? But at least Lincoln was the detective to show up, and she knew that he could be trusted. The problem was, Sawyer didn't know him and had serious trust issues.

Lincoln entered the room and approached Everly while keeping Sawyer in his line of sight. "It's good to see you again, Everly, though I'm sorry about the circumstances."

She shook his hand. "Lincoln, this is Sawyer Blackwood."

Lincoln shook Sawyer's hand. "It's nice to meet you."

Sawyer nodded but said nothing. "I'll leave you two alone."

He turned to walk away.

"Sawyer, wait. You might as well stay." She glanced at Lincoln to confirm this was okay.

"That's fine," Lincoln said. "In fact, I think it's a good idea. I have a few questions for him too."

She ignored the anger that flashed in Sawyer's eyes, and she was relieved that Lincoln had been looking at her, not Sawyer.

"Let's sit down."

She gestured to the sprawling living area and took a seat on the edge of the sofa. Sawyer joined her at the opposite end of the sofa, and Lincoln sat down in the chair in the corner.

"Why don't you tell me what happened today?" His grin was tenuous. "I know you've already told the officers who arrived on the scene—"

She held up her hand to stop him. "I know the drill, Lincoln."

Everly explained everything in detail as Lincoln listened intently and took notes.

"And you believe this wasn't some random act of road rage?"

"I don't know what I could have done to cause the reaction, but…um…" She fought the need to glance at Sawyer for his permission. "No. I don't think it was road rage."

"You're working as hired protection. Do you believe the incident is connected?"

"I don't know." *That's something for the police to find out.* She bit back those words.

Lincoln flipped to a new page. "Mr. Blackwood, why did you hire HPS to protect your niece?"

"Someone was following me."

"Did you report it?"

Sawyer crossed his arms and shrugged. "No. I hired protection for Layla."

Everly suspected that Lincoln did a great job biting

back his own words because Sawyer was more than obviously not willing to open up.

"Okay. Let me shift gears. Earlier today, you were searching for the driver of the truck that hit you."

Sawyer visibly stiffened but said nothing.

Had Lincoln learned of her inquiry into the police report?

Lincoln stared at him as if waiting for a response; when he got none, he looked at his notepad, then back up to Sawyer. "Were you able to locate him? Talk to him?"

"His neighbor told me he had loaded luggage and left—so, no, I wasn't able to talk to him."

"I wasn't able to talk to him, either, to question him after his initial statement to the officer on the scene after the accident, although he was informed to stick around." Lincoln stood. "Now he's missing. But we were able to learn where he was headed."

Everly stood too. "But he never made it?"

"I'm afraid not."

"What about the driver of the Tahoe that tried to force Everly off the road?" Sawyer asked, which surprised Everly. "Did you find him?"

"Not yet."

"Do you know who he is?"

"Not yet."

Because a corporation owned the vehicle. It took some digging to find the individual behind the wheel.

Lincoln tucked his notepad away. "I'm glad that you and Layla weren't seriously hurt, Everly. You know how to reach me when you or Mr. Blackwood are ready to open up about what's really going on here. I don't have all the facts, so I won't make any assumptions regarding the reason you've been hired to protect his niece, but there could be a connection. I know it and you know it." When he looked at her, he almost appeared wounded.

She walked him to the door, and he exited. She remained on the porch to see him out. "We'll contact you when there is something you need to know." It was all she could think to say.

"I'd like for you to let me be the judge of that." He held her gaze.

When she said nothing more, Lincoln nodded, then said, "Be careful. That guy's hiding something."

She crossed her arms after giving a little wave. She would neither deny nor confirm to Lincoln what he'd quickly suspected—and what she already knew as truth.

SEVEN

Sawyer scraped a hand down his face, hoping he could wipe away his expression. The police were asking questions, and it was only a matter of time before they asked more than he was willing to answer. In fact, he'd tempered his replies today and avoided providing complete answers. But Detective Mann was no fool.

He would probably find out more before confronting Sawyer with additional questions—and yeah, he would definitely be back to grill Sawyer.

Everly was still out on the porch so Sawyer paced and huffed.

What was she saying?

Why was she saying anything? Taking so long?

Maybe Detective Mann hadn't pressed Sawyer, but Everly wouldn't let him dodge her questions anymore. And he needed to make a decision. Before then, though, he needed clarity. He needed to push aside the surge of jealousy that had come out of nowhere. Sawyer had no right to feel that way, no claim on her, personally.

He had no doubt that Detective Mann was interested in Everly. Sawyer recognized that look in the man's eyes; but to the detective's credit, he didn't come on strong, if at all.

Sawyer had to keep busy. He had to do something. He headed to the kitchen and started preparing dinner before Everly did. He heard her step back inside and make a call on her cell phone. She kept her voice low, obviously wanting to keep her conversation private.

He respected that and wouldn't listen in—but man, he wanted to know what she could possibly be saying to someone after the detective's visit. Who had she called? But if he expected her to trust him, then he needed to also trust her. In fact, of all the people in his life, he trusted Everly the most. Was he making a mistake?

She entered the kitchen. "What are you doing?"

Without looking up from the onions and garlic he'd chopped and dropped into a skillet to sauté, he answered, "You told me to get on top of meal prep, so this is me, making dinner."

She leaned against the counter. "Smells good. What are we having tonight?"

He glanced at the ground beef on the counter. "Tacos. I hope that's okay."

"I love tacos. I can chop the veggies to go on top."

"Veggies?"

"You know—tomatoes, lettuce and onions. The cheese is already grated."

"Really, let me do it. You have other things to do."

"Right. I see what you're trying to do. You want me out of your hair and distracted. You're trying to get rid of me."

"Now, why would I do that?" But she had him pegged. And in spite of his personal fear of what came next, he smiled as he dumped the beef into the pan. It sizzled and the smell of onions and garlic with the meat made his mouth water. Cooking wasn't that hard, actually. He should have done this a long time ago and taught Layla to cook as well.

Grief struck his heart—in many ways, he'd failed his niece, even though he'd done his best. Now, with Everly's help, he saw that his best could be better.

"Oh, you and I both know." She pulled the vegetables out of the fridge and plopped them on the counter. Grabbed another cutting board and knife. "You don't want me to ask questions. And I would ask the same ones that Lincoln had, but I know you'll just tell me to trust you."

While relief should have surged through him that she wasn't going to grill him—at least not yet—that jealousy slivered through him again. "'Lincoln'? You go by first names?" He wanted to kick himself for asking.

"We worked together before. I told you that." She came up next to him and hovered too close.

They had almost kissed before Lincoln had *rudely* interrupted, and Sawyer should thank the guy for saving the day—saving Sawyer from making a colossal mistake, that is. Kissing her would put a huge hitch into this operation.

He stirred the sizzling meat so all the pink would turn brown.

"I didn't call him, Sawyer. I already told you that. But I'm glad it was Lincoln who showed up. HPS works with him a lot. But…outside of that…we also often investigate for clients who don't want the police involved. You wouldn't be the first."

He set the spatula down and turned to her. She wasn't fooling him. "Is that your way of asking me to tell you something more?"

Crossing her arms, she smiled, and totally disarmed him. He was prepared for her to pressure him, but she was using a different tactic altogether. Unfortunately, it was working. Her beautiful smile. That dimple in her left cheek.

And…he didn't look at her lips again. But he knew they were soft and pink and…so kissable. He lifted his gaze to meet hers.

She arched a brow and took a step back. "Don't worry, Sawyer. I'm not going to ask you anything you don't feel comfortable sharing, even though we usually make sure that our clients are…let's say, above board."

A pang shot through him. "You don't think I'm involved in something illegal?"

"I hope not. But I can't really know for sure. I…I don't know you."

He was surprised at how much her words hurt. "You know me, Everly."

But was that true? Sawyer wasn't sure he even knew himself.

"I *knew* you, Sawyer. But you're a much different man now. And I'm a different woman. We're both different people."

He nodded and focused back on finishing up their dinner. Everly quickly chopped the tomatoes and shredded lettuce. Put cheese and salsa in bowls.

She left them on the counter. "Now that's done, I'm going to check on the security cameras and go out and check the perimeter too. Given this second attack today, we need to be prepared for trouble."

"Agreed. I hired you because of suspicious activity— but with the physical attacks, my greatest fears have materialized." And he feared much more than what had already happened.

"You did the right thing, Sawyer. I'll be back in a few minutes."

All the same, he kept his cell on the counter so he could

see the security feeds. Hopefully, she wouldn't be attacked again. He realized she hadn't chopped up an onion, so he found one, placed it on the cutting board and started in, careful of the burn that was healing on his hand. But then he sliced into his finger and released a yelp.

Grabbing his bleeding finger, he ran it under the faucet. He'd need to wrap it up before he could finish. In the bathroom, he bandaged his finger and then stared at his reflection in the mirror, the bruise on his forehead. He looked like a complete wreck, which was how he felt inside.

If it wasn't for the concern for his clients' privacy and the delicate business he was in, he would have told Lincoln Mann everything, allowing the police to be fully involved. But as things stood, the last thing he needed was for the police to start digging into this.

He thought about the person who had followed him, who was probably also the same person who had been in the woods and who had tried to run Everly off the bridge.

Had someone learned of Sawyer's business dealings and the role he'd played in his clients' disappearances, and then wanted to expose him? On the other hand, why not simply approach him directly and ask him, talk to him, rather than attack him?

He ran a hand through his thick black hair, searching in the mirror for the man he once was. The man whom Everly knew.

She was a fantastic bodyguard now and, like she said, a different person. His biggest regret was that something more had not happened between them early on. But his life had been upended, and nothing could ever be the same again for him.

For us.

And now, since he kept the details from her, she'd become standoffish. She'd obviously gone through a lot since he knew her before. He'd seen it in her eyes when he'd told her about Paisley and recognized that look. Someone had terrorized her. He wanted to know more, but she wasn't opening up to Sawyer, and that was just as well. Neither of them had room in their lives for a relationship.

A knock came at the bathroom door. "Sawyer, you okay in there?"

He opened the door, and Everly took in his face; then her gaze dropped to his hand. "Let me guess…"

"It's nothing." He pushed past her.

She trailed him. "Everything outside was clear. I set the table."

Turning, he stared her down. "Thanks for your help, but I've got this. Let me do my job, and I'll let you do yours." Regretting his harshness, he sent her a smile, hoping to soften the words.

She glanced at his finger. "You're doing great, Sawyer. I shouldn't have been so hard on you about your domestic skills. Not everyone is good in the kitchen. Eating out, takeout, is all good. But I think you might have discovered a new talent, and you can add culinary skills to your list. Just…try not to chop your hand off next time."

Oh, she was cute. So cute. That dimple. Her shimmering hazel eyes.

And he should not be thinking of her in this way.

She stepped back. "Well, I'll get Layla so we can eat."

At least one of them held on to common sense.

When Everly approached Layla's room, the door was half-open. Knocking lightly, Everly peered inside, not wanting to intrude. Still, she'd been hired to protect the girl. Eyes widening in surprise, Layla stiffened when she saw

Everly. She quickly stuck her cell beneath her leg where she sat on the bed.

"Can I come in?"

"Sure. Is it time for dinner? Something smells good."

Everly moved into the room. "I just want to check the window. Make sure you leave it closed and locked, okay?" Sawyer had the alarm system bypass some of the windows so they could be opened to allow the cool Pacific Northwest air in during certain times. The windows had individual alarms.

Layla shrugged. "I'm not stupid."

"Of course you're not. I hadn't meant to imply that you were. Sometimes people forget." Then she angled her head. "Listen, I'm sorry about what happened today. Are you… Are you really okay? You rushed off to come to your room. I know you smiled and acted like it didn't affect you, but I know that it did."

Layla had been so shaken, and she couldn't have gotten over it so fast.

The girl pushed her hair behind her ears and nodded. "I was scared, but you kept us safe. So yeah. Sure. I'm still a little shaky. Who wouldn't be? But honestly… I'm used to this."

Wait. What? Every rushed forward and took the liberty of sitting next to Layla on the lavender bedspread covered with too many purple pillows. "What do you mean you're 'used to this'? Has someone tried to run you off the road before?"

Layla shrugged, continuing to keep her cell under her leg. "No, not that. But just… Uncle Sawyer has always been paranoid. Always overprotective, like he thinks someone is going to hurt us."

Oh. She was talking about that.

"You know why, though, don't you?" Everly knew she

shouldn't interfere and hoped she wasn't overstepping by having this conversation.

"Yes. I know that my mother and Uncle Sawyer were kidnapped, and it was a rough time for them. But that was a long time ago. Before I was born. So I don't know why we have to keep living like this."

"He's just trying to protect you."

Layla shrugged again and hung her head before glancing back up at Everly. The girl was hiding something, too; Everly sensed it. "I know. And I'm all he's got, so I try not to complain much."

"You're a good person, Layla. Sawyer is so fortunate to have you." Everly stood up from the bed and started for the door. When she glanced back, Layla once again stuck her cell beneath her leg. *Weird.* "Why don't you wash your hands and meet me in the kitchen. We can tell Sawyer how good it smells and tastes, and really encourage him."

She tossed Layla a big grin, hoping to disarm her and win her trust. Plus, the girl, like her uncle, needed the good moments in her life.

After the day they'd had, dinner was surprisingly uneventful—well, except for the fact that Sawyer's tacos were amazing. After eating, Layla had gone back to her room rather than hang around and chat.

Everly took a few minutes in the guest room and called Ayden to let him know how things were going. She informed him about today's incident and also that she had contacted the insurance company about her vehicle. Ayden agreed to trade out vehicles early in the morning. He would drop his off and pick hers up, then take care of the rest. But he sounded preoccupied with his own client, so she doubted he could devote much time to looking into a client who wanted to keep to himself.

Sawyer hadn't asked her to investigate—either officially or unofficially.

She sat on the bed and took in a deep breath. She needed to talk to him about her suspicions regarding Layla. But she had uncertainties about Sawyer too. He lived in a beautiful bungalow a few miles from town on an island surrounded with stunning views of Puget Sound. He was lonely and brooding and mysterious.

She knew she shouldn't get too close. Just do the job. Protect Layla until this was over.

Then get out.

But his secrets are drawing me in.

And at the end of the day, she was protecting him, too, though he might not believe he needed it.

She moved over to the dresser and stared at her pale complexion in the mirror. She'd never used much makeup; but seeing how plain she was now, she had the urge to take Layla to the mall to go makeup shopping after all.

You're being ridiculous.

She didn't need to try to look beautiful for Sawyer. She wasn't here for that.

Focus on something else.

The truck driver. Lincoln mentioned he was missing now. Maybe she could investigate on that behind the scenes to keep her hands on the pulse of things. Find out if the driver had been hired by someone and then who had hired him. Once she learned who was behind everything, this protection detail could be resolved.

And end.

She could get on with her life and away from Sawyer, who was clearly affecting her in the oddest ways.

Oh, bother. Lifting the brush from the dresser, she smoothed out her disheveled strands. She shouldn't be so hard on herself considering she'd been in an accident of sorts today, though the other guy suffered worse. Pinching her cheeks to bring out some color, she drew in a breath.

Time to face Sawyer.

Everly found him in the security-camera room. His gaze was intense as he stared at the woods and the area around the house. His brows furrowed, and he held a finger over his mouth as if deep in thought. She hated to interrupt him.

"If you want to get some rest, I'll take the first shift," he said without looking at her.

"Sawyer, we need to talk."

He lifted his gaze to meet hers, his dark eyes unreadable.

"This is about Layla."

The way he inhaled, lifted his shoulders, she suspected he believed she was overstepping. Before he could object, she dived right in.

"I think she's trying to hide who she's talking to on her cell. I'm not trying to spy on her or pry, but it made me think I should probably ask you if you've installed the appropriate apps on her cell to monitor her conversations. It's a good idea and gives you a way to protect her from predators. In the times we live in…" She didn't finish her sentence; Sawyer knew firsthand and didn't need her to go overboard explaining the dangers.

"I've put some protections on her cell phone, but I avoid stalker ware." He turned back to study the security monitors again. "My father was overbearing, and if I push too hard, then I'll just push her away."

"I understand where you're coming from. While you do a great job of protecting her—the security system, hiring me—you're leaving a big hole in your security. Layla is a young girl, which makes her vulnerable. Before you tell me that I'm overstepping, you've asked me to protect her, and I'm telling you I see a hole in the plan."

Sawyer pressed his hands against the desk and leaned on them, hanging his head. He sighed heavily before standing up straight again.

Then he looked at Everly. "Layla needs me to trust her if I want her trust in return."

"But, see, that's exactly what I'm saying. She is trustworthy and she adores you, but she's a child and someone could take advantage of her. The bottom line is that Layla trusts *you* to protect her." Everly sighed. "I get there's some conflict between trusting her and protecting her."

"Okay. I hear what you're saying."

"And?"

"I'll look into it."

"Good. Listen, I have an idea, but I want to make sure that my suggestion isn't going to interfere with your work. How is that going?"

He arched a brow. "My work is going fine. Why do you ask?"

"I haven't seen you work, really, since this started. I'm sure you're distracted."

"I'm between contracts. I probably won't take on a new project until this is over. Now, what was your idea?"

"Since Layla didn't get to go to the mall today and our plan now is to stick together, instead of her attending school tomorrow, how about we all go to the aquarium? That way, she gets out of the house, and you can spend some quality time with her. I'll be there as protection."

He studied her. "We'll take one day at a time. For now, that sounds like a plan."

"Okay, then. You good for the first shift?"

"Yes."

She glanced at her watch. "I'm setting my alarm for six hours, and then I'll relieve you."

He suddenly shifted, turning toward her, and his eyes roamed her face, taking her in as if he didn't already know her appearance. "Thank you for being here for us. For me. Layla adores you. I knew that she would."

And in his eyes, she thought she read that he shared that sentiment. Her heart spasmed.

He adores me too.

EIGHT

As they lingered near the octopus's tank, waiting for Layla, Sawyer leaned over and whispered, "Thank you for this idea."

Everly whispered back, "I thought she'd be excited to get out of the house on her day off from school. Even though it would be safer to stay at home, we're in a public place during a time when a few families with very young children are here—and I'm with you to protect you."

But today was turning out to be so much more than a simple outing. Sawyer had a feeling that Everly was concerned about Layla's mental and emotional health. The last few days had been traumatic for them all. And despite everything weighing on him, the aquarium was relaxing and some of the tension escaped his shoulders. His chest was less tight, and he could breathe easier.

Layla suddenly stared at her cell phone and frowned, distracted from the colorful underwater wildlife. Sawyer shared a look with Everly. He wished he would have held on to Layla's phone during their outing, like how they usually put them away during dinner so they could focus on each other.

"Oh, would you look at this," Everly said. "It's a manta ray petting pond. You stick your hand in the water, and they rush up and swim under your hand. How cool is that?"

Indeed. Sawyer wanted to try it too.

But Layla barely glanced up from her cell phone.

Sawyer pursed his lips. He fought back the desire to confiscate her cell phone for the remainder of their time together. But Layla was acting completely normal from what he'd seen of the world out there—everyone absorbed in their technology. Him included.

Should he? Or shouldn't he? He approached his niece, and she slowly looked up at him.

"What?" she asked.

"I'll make a deal with you." He held up his cell phone.

She angled her head and narrowed her eyes. "I'll need to know what the deal is before I agree to anything."

He bit back a smile. He could just take the cell from her, but he wanted her cooperation. "I want to spend time with you, but someone else has got your attention and is distracting you. How about I agree to put my cell away and not look at it or answer calls, and you do the same? Let's focus on what's right in front of us."

This moment in time. *We don't know what tomorrow will bring.*

Layla hesitated.

"Come on. Please?" Sawyer turned his cell phone off.

She released a dramatic huff. "I guess I can do that." She turned her cell off too. "But only for a few minutes."

Parenting—even though he wasn't her father, he was still her parent in a manner of speaking—was the hardest job he'd ever had. Maybe there was a book he could pick up.

Parenting for Dummy Uncles.

Sawyer thought back to Everly's words about Layla trying to hide whom she was talking to. He wasn't sure there was anything to it, but maybe she was right, and he should install an app to keep track of her conversations. He wasn't entirely sure what was available and how much privacy he should give her.

Whatever he did was for her protection.

Or he could try harder to earn her trust.

Like now. He held his arm out, and Layla came in close. He wrapped it around her shoulder, and together they walked over to view the manta rays swimming in circles around the pool.

"You wanna pet one?" He released her and let his hand hover over the water.

She shrugged. "I'll watch you do it first."

He thrust his hand under the water. Sure enough, a manta ray swam under his palm, and he felt the silky texture of skin. "It's soft," he said.

"Says here their skin is covered with mucus." Layla laughed when he jerked his hand out of the water. "But I want to feel it."

She stuck her hand in, and her smile was beautiful, just like her mother's. He didn't want to think about Paisley at this moment because he needed to enjoy this. He thought of her mantra.

"Life is not about waiting for the storm to pass. It's about learning how to dance in the rain."

I'm learning, sis. I'm trying and learning. This moment might be what you meant.

He glanced at Everly before turning his gaze back to the manta rays. Though she kept a straight face, her eyes smiled. Respect swam in her beautiful hazel gaze, causing warmth to spread through his body. Everly's presence, her responses, affected him more than he wanted to admit. He wanted to wrap his arm around Everly, too, like they were one big happy family.

What would it be like to have her in the family?

Hold on, there. I'm a long way from being able to commit to a relationship.

But his earlier words to Layla came back to him… *Let's focus on what's right in front of us.*

Everly. However brief, she was back in his life.

He had a feeling that Paisley would approve.

I can't. Not yet. Not now… He couldn't hurt her again.

They moved over to the next exhibit, Northwest Waters.

"It's a huge tank. One hundred thousand gallons filled with sea life and anemones," Layla told them, paraphrasing the information she was reading.

Sawyer stood back a bit to take in the massive twenty-four-foot-wide and ten-foot-tall window. He could see their reflections in the glass at this angle. Everly stepped back behind him and away from the aquarium. Something in her eyes and the way she had stiffened set off alarms in his head.

He moved closer to Layla to wrap his arm once again over her shoulder to protect her. That's all he wanted to do. But maybe his niece would be safer if she was far away from him. The incident yesterday on the bridge proved that she had now been targeted, too, because of her proximity to him.

Something to do with his father's past?

Something to do with his past in the military and business overseas?

But more likely to do with his present.

Everly circled them, her eyes searching the aquarium. He got the feeling that at any moment, she was going to pull out her gun in this very public place.

He approached. "What's going on?"

"We should leave now," Everly said.

"What? Why?" Layla asked.

He'd held on to hope that they could have a few moments to enjoy without the constant fear of danger. He'd wanted to spend time with Layla…and Everly too.

"I'm disappointed too," he said to his niece. "I'll bring you back when it's safe to do so."

"When will that be?" Layla shrugged out of his arm.

"Just a few minutes ago, you acted like you could care less about being here when you were texting." He wished he hadn't said the words.

"We can talk about it later." Everly ushered them toward the exit.

One of the larger tanks suddenly exploded, glass shattering outward, pushed by hundreds of thousands of gallons of water. They'd already started for the door, but that didn't save them from being doused.

Screams reverberated as water, along with fish— and, Sawyer just now realized, dangerous electric eels— washed across the floor. People ran. A woman fell, along with her small child. Sawyer scooped up the child and assisted the woman. He glanced at Everly, who ushered Layla forward and out the door with only a glance at him.

Good. Layla was to be protected, even if it meant Sawyer must be left behind.

He looked around to see if anyone else needed assistance, but most everyone had gotten out. This was in the middle of a school day, after all, and only a handful of people were here. He was thankful the crowd was small. But what had happened?

He wanted to linger so he could find out if someone was behind what had happened to the tank. Aquarium employees and volunteers rushed forward and worked to save the sea life that could die outside of the water.

"What happened?"

"Sir, please leave the area. We apologize for the inconvenience."

This had to have been deliberate. Everly must have sensed something before it happened. Sawyer slowly moved toward the exit and looked around. In the shadows on the far side of the big exhibit hall, he spotted someone watching and then suddenly disappear. The person was wearing black and not the bright turquoise blue of an employee but had entered an employees-only area.

He took off after them, splashing through the water, instead of toward the exit.

"Sir, where are you going? Please exit the premises!"

He sidestepped the squirming eels and hopped onto the dais as he heard electricity buzzing from them. He hoped the workers knew what they were doing. He raced toward the employees-only door and shoved through. The hallway was empty; probably everyone was in the exhibit, trying to save the sea life.

A door slammed and he followed the sound. Another exit out of the building.

Sawyer raced through the exit and around to the front. The vehicle Everly now drove—her brother's—peeled out of the parking lot but then swerved toward him. It squealed to a stop, and he jumped in. "I saw him leave out this exit. Did you see him?"

"I did. We're going to follow him. He's in a Cadillac." She sped out of the parking lot.

"Don't let him get away."

"We got the license plate number. Call it in," she said. "Call Detective Mann and tell him what's happened."

Could he do that? Did he really want the police involved? But they were already involved, and he was fighting a losing battle.

"Sawyer, do it. Please."

"You don't understand what's at stake."

She raced down the road, weaving in and out of traffic, to follow the Cadillac.

"You might have your priorities messed up," she said.

"Will the two of you stop?" Layla sounded near tears. "You're scaring me!"

Sawyer turned on his cell and made the call.

Everly was right: Layla was Sawyer's priority. But he could put others at risk with this one call because this time, he would have to explain that someone had followed them and somehow rigged a tank to shatter.

And he would have to tell them why.

God, I don't know why.

But he had his suspicions.

While Everly wanted to continue following their assailant, it wasn't her job to chase him down.

Back at the aquarium, she'd listened to her instincts that told her someone was watching. The feeling had caused goose bumps to crawl over her arms. Not only had someone been watching, but they had also meant to cause harm. When the aquarium had shattered, her focus had been on keeping Layla safe.

She remembered that glance back at Sawyer, who was helping a woman and her young child—and that's all she could offer him. A glance. She had rushed Layla to the vehicle, then sped toward the front of the building, hoping, praying that Sawyer would rush out.

Especially when she'd spotted a familiar-looking guy—wearing all black and acting suspicious—running from the back of the building. He had been up to no good.

He was big, too, like the guy in the alley. Like the guy who had grabbed her in the woods. And now, he was driving the Cadillac. Weird. The Cadillac had been following Sawyer, he'd said, when the truck hit him. It appeared that at least two people were working together on coming after Sawyer or the person he loved—Layla.

Inside the aquarium, she had tried to take a picture, but they had all turned off their cells, and it took too long for her phone to boot up; by the time it finally did, the tank had exploded.

Finding the guy, tracking him down, could go a long way in protecting them.

But this car-chase business was dangerous for those around them and dangerous for the occupants of the car.

She slowed and moved with the flow of the traffic.

"What are you doing?" Sawyer shouted.

But she kept her voice even. "It's too dangerous. We have the license plate. You contacted Lincoln."

"I left him a voice mail."

"I'm saying, let *him* find this guy. That's his job."

His jaw worked, and his white knuckles attested to his tight grip on the handle. She understood that he wanted to chase after this guy who had caused so much trouble, but not with Layla in the car. Once he calmed down, he would understand that she was right.

She shouldn't have engaged, but she'd gotten caught up in the chase too. After all, he was *right there. So close.*

Too close.

"I didn't see anyone following us. I didn't see the Cadillac. And that's on me." She wanted to talk more about the situation, but not in front of Layla. The girl had powered up her cell phone again and was texting, but she would still listen to their discussion. Everly might suggest they take her to school since the aquarium visit hadn't worked out, or even to the mall since she hadn't gotten that trip yesterday, but clearly someone was bent on getting to them no matter where they showed up.

Someone had followed them or tracked them.

She had to admit that she might not be the best person for this job after all, even though Sawyer believed she was. Or maybe he, too, was having doubts. Everly concentrated on the road as well as the mirrors as she drove across the bridge and headed down the rural road toward Sawyer's bungalow on the island. No one was following them now—as far as she could tell.

Then again, no one needed to follow them.

Sawyer's home wasn't a secret. Someone had already been near the property, watching.

Depending on what Lincoln told them about today's incident and depending on the answers Sawyer gave to her questions, they should seriously consider going to a safe house.

For Layla's sake.

Everly might even suggest Layla go into protective custody with HPS or even another entity while she and Sawyer faced off with this guy. She was all for waiting for the bad guy to come to them at the house.

Bring it on.

By the time she pulled into the driveway and into the garage, the gray clouds had turned pewter. The region was usually gray and rainy this time of year, but the clouds seemed especially dark today—to go with her current mood.

Sawyer had checked the cameras on his cell before they even steered into the driveway.

She turned off the ignition and looked at him. "Well?"

"All is well at Casa Blackwood." He sent her a grin.

Was he trying to lighten the mood for Layla's sake? In the back seat, the girl smiled but hadn't looked up from her cell phone. Whether she was smiling because of what

Sawyer said or something going on in her texting world was hard to know.

"We need to talk." Everly pressed her hand over his and squeezed. That was becoming her mantra with him.

He nodded, understanding she meant later.

"In the meantime," she added, "I can whip up a batch of brownies." *You know, to make up for what happened today.* But what was she thinking? Layla wasn't five.

He shook his head. "Nice try. But I need you on guard duty because I make spaghetti for dinner."

"While I can multitask as well as the next woman, you're absolutely right." That's why he had hired her. So what was wrong with her? Why was she trying to play another role in his life?

From the back seat, Layla suddenly leaned forward so that she was between them. "I'll make the brownies, but you're still making pasta, Uncle Sawyer."

Everly shared a look and a smile with Sawyer.

They climbed out of the vehicle, and she announced she would clear the house first, even though the cameras had told them it was safe. Once the house was cleared, she moved to the outside. No one appeared to be lurking nearby.

She stared off into the dark woods surrounding the property. At least the tree line started at a distance, and the house was far enough away that even if someone was watching her at this moment, he wouldn't pose an immediate threat. Okay, well, that wasn't completely true if he was an expert marksman with a sniper rifle. The thought of someone hiding in the woods unsettled her. The cameras were good, but they didn't catch everyone, as they had learned the other day.

A more secure location would be better.

Lord, please protect us—and please, if it's Your will, help me talk Sawyer into going to a safe house.

She'd never been in such a precarious position with a client before. Sawyer and Layla were both in danger, but he so far hadn't fully cooperated with police or asked for their involvement because he was adamant about maintaining privacy.

I hope Sawyer's reasons are good ones.

With one last look at the dark clouds that were about to dump on them, she headed back into the house.

Wearing an apron with a few splotches of tomato sauce, Sawyer met her at the door and closed it behind her. Armed the system. "We're in a flood warning tonight. I doubt anyone will try anything."

"I hope you're right." The aroma of Italian food wrapped around her.

She could see brownies baking in the oven too, but Layla wasn't in the kitchen.

He was trying hard, doing what he could to make the best of the situation and to be the best parenting uncle he could. Everly would give him stars for that.

In the meantime, she would do her best, too, by gathering more intel. Threat analysis would go a long way in this protection detail. She just needed to convince Sawyer.

She intended to find out what was going on—for real. The truth he kept to himself—before it was too late.

NINE

Watching the sideways rain come down in sheets, Sawyer peered out the window. Though he wasn't concerned about a tornado in this region, the high or straight-line winds could still cause damage…and death. Only two trees grew near the house, and their branches scraped across the shingles. One against the window. He prayed nothing came crashing through the roof.

Everly claimed she would rest a few hours, then come to relieve him, and he hadn't argued, but he had no intention of sleeping tonight. Not with someone bent on getting to him and going through Layla if he had to. Not with the storm…

But that was the least of his worries. He'd told Everly that no one would try anything on this stormy night. He had a feeling that he had been completely wrong on that point. The tingles across his skin, his instincts, were making a liar out of him. Maybe he was being paranoid and overreacting, but he couldn't risk it.

Squeezing the grip of his 9 mm pistol, which he held down at his side, he moved over to peer out another window. The skies were black. He had to completely rely on the cameras, and they wouldn't work that well on a stormy night when bushes and trees were moving with the wind. In fact, his cameras were lighting up on his cell. He might have to spend the night in the security room.

He had the best security he could get based on the threat level, which, at the time the cameras and alarm system had been installed, hadn't been as significant as it was now. He'd done it as a precaution.

And because we were kidnapped before.

Maybe he should be well over the kidnapping that had happened more than a decade ago by now, but the nightmares still plagued him.

A couple of hours later, winds still lashed the house, keeping Sawyer uncomfortable. He'd made a huge pot of coffee—the good, strong stuff—and settled in a chair. He didn't want to get so comfortable that he fell asleep but pacing and glancing out the windows all night would do him no good.

Why do I still sense someone is watching? Or am I letting the fear get the best of me?

He heard soft footfalls and glanced up to see Everly approaching. Earlier in the day, in the car, she'd told him they needed to talk. He'd known then what she would ask him, and he'd been dreading that conversation all evening. Now she wanted answers.

God, what do I tell her?

Surprisingly, Everly didn't approach him but instead moved over to the window. He couldn't help but notice— not for the first time—how gracefully she moved. Her shiny brown hair fell to her shoulders instead of how she usually pinned it up, and he knew from experience that the strands were soft to the touch.

Maybe he shouldn't be making such observations, but his defenses were fried on the personal front. All his protective strength was focused on this situation—the very real threat of physical danger. He had no will to fight his once-buried-but-now-rekindled emotions when it came to Everly.

Lifting the heavy curtain, she peered out into the night. He took in her trim athletic figure and spotted the gun at her side. She was a beautiful woman in every way—inside and out—stunning and intimidating at the same time.

An exotic action figure, and that intrigued him.

She turned to look at him, her hazel eyes holding his gaze.

Does she know I was thinking about her?

He had no will to hide that truth from her.

But another truth pushed aside his longing for her: they couldn't be together. Sawyer had no room in his life for emotional entanglements, and he knew that he would only hurt them both again if he allowed his feelings to go anywhere. That is, if she even felt the same way about him. She was more likely to reject him because he'd hurt her so deeply in the past. He couldn't blame her for that.

He only blamed himself.

"Call me crazy, but I think someone might actually be out in that storm." She went to sit on the sofa near his chair.

"You're not crazy. I sense it too." He glanced at his gun on the side table.

Everly's eyes snagged on the Glock, then riveted back to him. She pursed her lips and studied him. He suspected she was measuring her words, and now was their time to have the talk.

"My brother Ayden was with the DSS—Diplomatic Security Services—before he came back from overseas and founded Honor Protection Specialists."

Sawyer shut his laptop to listen.

"His job was to protect VIPs, state department heads,

country leaders at embassies. One of the most important aspects of his job was threat analysis. One of the most important aspects of *any* protection detail is threat analysis. Prevention. I know you understand where I'm going with this."

He shifted forward in his chair. A nasty gust of wind rocked the house, and the heavy tree branch slammed hard. A shudder rocked through him. Everly jerked and glanced around the ceiling.

"I'm not sure this is the best time to talk." He slid forward, pressed his hand over his gun.

"There is never going to be a good time. I need to know what you know, Sawyer. I need to know who you think is behind this."

"I've told you, I don't know."

"But you have suspicions you haven't shared with me or with Detective Mann."

He shrugged. "My suspicion means nothing."

"Then let's start with what you do for a living as a consultant. What kind of imports and exports do you specialize in?"

"I only need you to protect Layla." *Please don't make me fire you.*

"I'm trying to make you understand this is part of protecting her."

The last bodyguard wouldn't have asked questions, but Sawyer didn't think arguing that point would do any good.

He bolted from the chair, grabbed his gun and moved to the window to glance out into the darkness. In other parts of the country, this storm would be accompanied with a lot more lightning, which would light up the surroundings here and there. He wished that would happen now so he could see.

Who is watching?

"I know I'm asking you to tell more than you're willing to share. Sawyer, it's me. You know me. Please trust me."

If only she knew just how much he wanted to tell her, but he couldn't risk it. Or could he? If he could trust anyone, he could trust Everly. She might actually be the one person he could trust to look into why someone had followed him and tried to kill him.

"There's nothing to tell, Everly. Too many variables make it impossible to know."

"If you won't tell the police, you make it impossible to catch this guy."

"I've told them what I know." He sighed, feeling deflated, the fight going out of him. "For all I know, this could have to do with Dad's business. He's deceased and someone else runs the company, but who knows. People find all kinds of reasons to go after someone. Maybe Dad wronged someone and they're torturing me for some reason."

"And your *own* business?"

She just wouldn't let it go, would she? He couldn't blame her for that either. He shouldered the burden of all the blame.

"I don't see how that could be related." True. He couldn't see how. No one knew Sawyer's connection to his clients. But he was leaning toward his covert endeavors being the link. "I also worked overseas as a contractor. I don't see that this is related, though, because it's just this one guy. I'd love to finally take him down."

"Two guys. Someone drove the Cadillac the day you were hit. Someone else watched from the alley."

"Okay. Two guys. But I'm guessing only one person is actually behind it, calling the shots."

"That's fair. But my point is that we both want to take

him down. I wanted to follow him, but I stopped because it wasn't safe for Layla. She isn't safe here now, in the house, and you know I'm right. After this storm, we need to move her to a safe house."

Pain lanced his chest. He'd tried so hard to protect her from ever experiencing the nightmare he and her mother had gone through. While moving to a safe house wasn't being kidnapped, the same feelings of being held captive could traumatize Layla. Then again, as long as it was with people she knew and trusted...

Everly was suddenly next to him, pressing her hand gently on his arm. Electricity and warmth surged through his veins and rippled over his skin. He closed his eyes.

Please don't do that...

Then Everly spoke softly. "She's already been through so much, Sawyer. Too much. Let's keep her safe until this is over."

He pulled his gaze from her and stepped away before he made the mistake of pulling her into his arms. For too long, he'd let his mind think about her as a woman and not as Layla's protector. He should never had strayed off the path.

As for safe houses...

After what had happened to Paisley, he majored in getting people to safety.

God, why am I failing to do the one thing I'm good at? Why am I failing the most important person—people— in my life?

Because Everly meant everything to him too.

Everly understood his need to put space between them. She shouldn't have touched his arm—he obviously felt the connection, the attraction. She'd seen it in his eyes, to go on top of his obvious frustration at her questions.

She'd pushed him for answers, and she sensed that she only needed to continue to push gently. He was close to telling her the secrets he kept.

The secrets that so obviously—at least to her—were putting Layla in danger.

Gripping his gun at his side, he turned and walked away toward the kitchen, then down the short hallway to the security room.

He hadn't given her an answer.

She went the other direction, also gripping her gun. She checked all the windows and the back door. Alarm systems weren't failproof.

While the storm lashed at the house, emotions tormented Everly. With Sawyer pulling back—emotionally speaking—she felt the absence of their connection. They weren't together like before, but being back in his life in this pressure cooker situation was having an unexpected effect on her. Or maybe she should have expected that her heart would be vulnerable to him—the man she'd loved so fully and deeply. The man who had ripped her heart out.

Even though he'd hurt her in the past, she couldn't really hold what happened against him. He'd been damaged. Broken. But now he had picked up the pieces to make a new life for himself, and she admired him all the more.

He'd definitely filled out with his broad shoulders, sturdy chest and solid core. His eyes had grown even more intense and his jaw stronger, hair thicker... Okay, now she was just going overboard.

Still, he'd built a new life, but it was a life that had circled back around to include danger to him and those he loved.

The tree branch struck the roof again and startled her. She was letting herself get worked up.

Get a grip, Everly.

She glanced out the window. No way would she be able to sleep tonight, and she didn't think Sawyer would either. She texted Ayden about securing a safe house for tomorrow—at least it would be ready, if she could talk Sawyer into it.

Another glance out the window and a strike of lightning, and she was nearly convinced she'd seen someone out there. Maybe she was imagining it. Who would be out in this storm?

That's it.

She was going out into the storm, and she would find and take down this guy.

She stopped at the back door and grabbed her coat.

Sawyer came out of the security-camera room. "What do you think you're doing?"

"Catching this guy will go a long way to end this. He's out there. Someone is out there."

Coat donned, Glock ready, she reached for the alarm system. Sawyer caught her elbow and whirled her around to face him. He gripped both her arms and stood so close, she could feel the fear pouring off him, and it nearly knocked her back.

She opened her mouth to speak.

The lights suddenly went out.

Everly stiffened.

"You check on Layla." Sawyer released her arms. "I'll check the breaker box."

They both turned on their flashlights.

Everly moved through the house and down the hallway. She peeked in on Layla, prepared for the girl to be frightened in her bed, but she found her sleeping soundly. Everly wished she could sleep so soundly during a never-ending deluge.

Everly glanced around the room, looking at the window. She moved quietly and checked to make sure it remained locked, then sneaked back out.

It was probably the storm that had knocked the power out. But if someone was outside, they could use this as an opportunity. She left the bedroom door cracked, but before she stepped out of the room, the sound of glass shattering somewhere in the house startled her.

The alarm didn't go off.

Layla gasped and sat up, her eyes wide with fear. She shoved the cell under her pillow. Had she been pretending to sleep? Everly lifted her weapon, prepared to defend and protect.

"What's happened?" Layla asked.

"I don't know." She didn't want to scare the girl, but… "Slip into some jeans. Get your shoes on."

In case they needed to get out of here.

"Isn't it just the storm? Why do you have your gun out?"

"Please, Layla. Do as I ask."

Layla scrambled from the bed, yanked the jeans from off the floor and slipped into them. She stuck her cell in her pocket. Everly needed to check on the noise, but she didn't want to leave Layla.

"Come on," she whispered. She led Layla to the bathroom in the hallway. "Stay here until I get back. Do not open this door. Get down in the bathtub and hide."

"I'm scared." Layla stepped into the tub and sat down. She pulled the shower curtain forward. "Hurry, Everly."

"I promise I'll be back to get you. Stay quiet." Everly shut the bathroom door.

She moved quietly to the end of the hallway.

Sawyer moved through the house toward her, his flashlight leading the way. "Stay here and protect Layla. Where is she?"

"In the bathroom, hiding in the tub," she whispered.

"I'll check the house." He left her in the hallway.

Be careful, Sawyer.

Once they were sure there was an intruder, she would call 911. Concern rippled through her.

Sawyer's system was set up to run on batteries in case of a power outage. Maybe a tree branch had hit the glass. Regardless, if the window had its own alarm or it was set up on the main system, the alarm should be going off. Setting off the alarm would automatically send an alert to the police. The fact that it wasn't going off could mean someone had tampered with the alarm system.

She had one hand on her gun and a finger on the emergency button on her cell. What was she doing? Better the police came out and learn she had made a mistake than to not call when help was needed. She contacted dispatch and asked for assistance, then ended the call. She needed to focus on the protective detail so that seriously bad things didn't happen while they waited on the police to arrive.

Everly waited and listened, fighting the need to pace. Hating that she was relegated to standing guard in the hallway. She'd prefer to search the house and take down the intruder. But protecting Layla was her priority.

God, please let there not be an intruder.

But even as she prayed, she sensed that someone had entered the house. She stepped into the shadows and aimed her gun to be ready. She had to be careful not to shoot Sawyer.

He crept back to the hallway and signaled—military style—that two intruders had entered the house.

She nodded to Sawyer that she was ready, and by his

stance, she suspected he had been preparing for this day ever since he'd been kidnapped years ago.

Between the two of them, they had both developed the skill set to defend themselves.

And protect Layla.

TEN

Sawyer hated that things had come to this. Men invading his home. His safe place.

Muffled gunshots resounded through the home. Suppressors. They were using suppressors.

Sawyer dived behind the sofa and tried to wrap his mind around this insane scenario.

Everly hid behind the plush chair that now had holes in it. She signaled that she was okay, then disappeared from his line of sight.

His gun ready, he remained stock-still and quiet.

When a pair of boots came into view beneath the sofa, Sawyer knew he would soon be discovered. Time to go on the offensive. Sawyer tackled the man to the ground. He received a knee to his gut. An elbow to his side.

And he delivered as good as he got.

Pain ignited at the side of his head. He crumpled to the floor and tried to scramble to his feet. But the intruder was on top of him and trying to force his gun at Sawyer's face. Sawyer held him off, working to push it away.

"Who. Are. You?" He ground out the words, grunting with the effort to stay alive.

Anger coursed through him.

"What. Do. You. Want?"

He got no answer. He growled and squeezed the man's wrist as he twisted his face away from a direct shot. Fear for Everly, for Layla, rocked through him.

I have to live. Layla needs me. I'm all she has!

He knocked the gun out of the man's hand, then landed punches to his gut and nose. He tore the man's mask off, but it was too dark to get a good look. Sawyer rolled the man over just as a bullet whizzed by his head, and he once again dived behind the sofa. He couldn't return fire because he might hit Everly.

But he spotted her obvious silhouette when lightning flashed and briefly brightened the room.

She stood with a wide stance, aiming her gun, then shot at one of the men.

He tumbled out the shattered window. Sawyer crawled out from behind the sofa, trying to ignore the pain as he stumbled back and attempted to right himself. The man he'd taken down was gone.

"They're getting away!" Everly shouted.

Eyes burning, nose bleeding, Sawyer shook off the daze. "Stay here and protect Layla. I'm going after them."

He dashed out the door and into the raging wind and lashing rain. Sawyer spotted the figures racing toward the cover of the trees. Adrenaline coursing through his body, the pain from the fistfight faded, and he flew across the wide expanse of his five acres and toward the woods. He had to catch those men.

Wind drove the rain into his face, and it stabbed like daggers.

I must protect my family.

They melted into the woods, and darkness closed in on him, but he pushed toward those trees.

Sawyer brandished his gun again. He needed to defend himself—once he found them, that is.

And he needed to catch these guys.

Or at least one of them.

He sloshed through deep puddles across the acreages until he made it into the shadow of the trees. There, he paused against a thick-trunked cedar and caught his breath.

Were they waiting for him? Had they wanted to draw him out here alone?

He might have been a fool to follow them out—after all, he was the one they were after. If they had any skills, they would turn back and trap him.

Shining his flashlight, he spotted blood on the ground, already being washed away. Nope. They couldn't fight him now. One assailant needed to assist the other one.

Tree bark exploded next to his head, and he ducked and rolled. Caught his breath. Heart pounding, he crawled over behind another tree.

He hadn't really thought they would circle back. Not with one of them seriously injured. Sawyer moved to another tree and turned his flashlight off, then started carefully heading in the direction he thought they'd gone. But without the light, he could hardly see where he was going. Still, he had to try to follow them. These woods went on for about twenty more acres, but it was likely that the men who'd come through them to his property would take the shortest route out.

To the road.

Sawyer continued moving through the woods, making slow progress. Hopping over slick moss-covered logs. Weaving in and out of underbrush, ferns and then over rocks and around a few large boulders. An engine roared to life near the road.

Yep. As he suspected.

He rushed forward in time to see the rear lights of a

vehicle disappearing. He failed to get a license plate number, but it wasn't the Cadillac—that much he could tell. It was a large SUV. *A Hummer, maybe?* Just too dark to tell.

Soaking wet, he let the failure dig deep and cut through him. He tucked his damp gun away and made a beeline through the woods to the house. The police already had the license plate number of the Cadillac as well as the car that had flipped at the bridge. So at least they had those leads to follow.

Sawyer kept his head up and remained alert as the rain seemed to slow. The forecast had predicted much more, so he would enjoy what would be a short reprieve. He tried not to slump under the weight of the last few days as he pushed through the woods.

Whoever was after him was taking bigger risks every day.

And tonight, they had invaded his home. What did they want?

To kill him? Scare him? If he was the one they were after—and he had to believe that was true—then why try to run Everly and Layla off the bridge?

God, please help me to stop the insanity.

The lights were still off when he stepped through the door. He crept through the house. Could he know whether the two guys he chased were the only ones? Had someone taken the opportunity to come inside and attack while he was gone?

Fear snaked around his neck and squeezed. He wanted to call out for Everly and Layla, but he kept quiet as he crept forward, fearing the worst for those he loved.

Loved.

There it was again.

That word that included thoughts of Everly.

The muzzle of a gun pressed against his temple.

* * *

Heart in her throat, Everly stepped away before the man could turn to disarm her.

"Sawyer…" She could barely croak out the words. She dropped the gun to her side. "I'm sorry. I had to be sure it was you."

God, what am I doing?

What should be a simple protection detail was getting out of control.

Breathing hard, Sawyer faced her. Though she kept the flashlight pointed down, it provided enough light so she could see he was dripping wet. That shouldn't surprise her, but he had to be freezing.

She grabbed a throw blanket from the sofa and tossed it over him.

"Layla?"

"Here." She stepped out of the shadows. "I was still hiding in the tub, but I heard it was you."

"What happened?"

"I lost them, that's what. They got away."

"Not before I shot one of them in the leg."

"They'll be heading to a hospital. To the ER. He was bleeding badly," Sawyer said. "Did you call 911?"

"Yes. But I have bad news. Help has to come from the other side of the island because the road is flooded, so they have to take the long way around."

"If the road out of here is flooded, then…" He pressed a fist to his lips and paced. "Then those men who broke into the house can't get out either. That means they have to come back this direction."

Sawyer's expression said it all: he didn't like the idea. They could try something again—or one of them could, if the other got the bleeding under control. They could know the police would take too long, and they could try again.

"Whatever happens to those men, Sawyer, we can't stay here. The power's out. The alarm system is down. Maybe it was the storm, or maybe those men did something. But it doesn't matter. We can't stay."

His dark look spoke volumes. "I agree."

And for once, they could see eye to eye—but it had come at a high price. "I've already arranged for a safe house," she said. "Gather what you need, and we're getting out of here."

Everly pulled Layla to her in a big hug, and the girl wrapped her arms around her. Warmth flooded her. She didn't usually become so attached to clients, but this was different. Her client was a young girl who needed more than a bodyguard with a gun—she needed emotional support. And apparently, Layla had bonded with Everly.

Sawyer hadn't missed the exchange, and he held Everly's gaze for so long, she wanted to question him about what he was thinking. He seemed to be searching the deepest parts of her.

Again.

"You heard her, Layla," he said. "Grab one small bag. We need to move, and fast."

"I'll go with you," Everly said.

"No, that's okay," she said. "I got it."

"For your protection."

Layla frowned, but Everly followed her down the dark hallway, guiding them with her flashlight. She kept her gun close.

In the bedroom, Everly shone the flashlight around. "There. I see a small backpack in the closet."

Everly started for it, but Layla beat her to it. She snatched the backpack up.

"Stuff it with a few toiletries and an extra pair of clothes. We can get more of what you need. Just get what you need for tonight."

"But I—"

"Nothing in here is worth your life. In fact, get whatever you can grab in two minutes because we're leaving in three."

Layla started huffing and puffing and pressing stuff into her bag. More stuff. The bag already had junk inside.

"Oh, honey. It's already packed." She stared at Layla.

"I never unpacked from a sleepover."

"Okay, well, pull out the dirty clothes and put some clean ones in, and let's go."

Layla had to be dramatic, but the girl was scared too. Everly would be patient and show compassion.

Layla slipped on shoes and put her backpack on.

Everly nodded. "Good." Then she led Layla out of her room, stopping by the room she'd been using and grabbing her own duffel.

At Layla's questioning look, she said, "It's always packed. I'm always ready for a fast departure."

"Or escape," Layla whimpered, then stood tall. "I'm sorry. This is just…"

Sawyer joined them. "You ready?"

"Yes. Let's get out of here." They hurried through the house. "I hate leaving it like this," Everly said, "but your lives are more important."

He ushered them out into the garage. "The rain could do some damage through those broken windows, but it's too dangerous to stay and fix them. We'll meet the police here in the morning."

She hid her shock at his words. The police? He'd been so adamant about keeping them out of what was going on. Still, she could understand now that his haven had been invaded, he was seeing reason.

"Let's take my car," she said. "Your rental has a low clearance. If there's flooding, mine is higher and would be better." And that was only because she was using Ayden's big-wheeled Suburban.

Sawyer didn't argue and opened the back for Layla to climb in. "Fine, but I'll drive. I know my way around the island."

He backed out of the driveway and pulled out onto the road, heading in the opposite direction from the bridge, toward where the help was supposed to come from; maybe they could meet the police.

"I'll call the locals and let them know we've had to leave, but they should still check the area for the men. That we'll be back in the morning to talk to them at the house. Check the hospitals for someone who was shot. Of course, they do that anyway, but I'm letting them know that I shot someone."

And normally, the police would want her to stay right there to wait for them and answer questions about an active shooting incident. But in their current predicament, waiting was too risky.

The night was dark and stormy and dangerous. Everly remained professional, and she would see Sawyer and Layla through.

But... God, I need some hope in this situation. Please, just let me get them someplace safe, warm and dry tonight.

ELEVEN

Gripping the steering wheel, Sawyer peered through the windshield at the small circle of light the headlights created. The wipers worked overtime.

Sawyer's heart pounded.

Their lives depended on him getting them away from the danger. He had never been more grateful that he'd brought Everly into this. He couldn't imagine keeping Layla safe all on his own. If his father had taken that step years ago, then he and Paisley might have been spared the trauma of being abducted, being kidnapped, and kept in a dark room. A basement crawling with bugs and rodents. After it was over, he thought the nightmares would never end.

Paisley had been the one to concoct the plan while they were in the room. She determined that once they were free, they would leave Seattle. Leave their father in every way possible. It seemed harsh to him now that he thought of it, but at the time, he and Paisley had been protecting each other. And then, she'd gotten married to the wrong man, and Sawyer had joined the army and ended up overseas.

"Watch out!" Everly shouted and gripped the dash.

He swerved, barely missing a deep puddle flooding the road. Water sprayed the windows on both sides.

"Uncle Sawyer?"

"What, honey?"

"Do we need to worry that someone is going to follow us?"

Maybe. "You're safe with us, Layla. You don't need to worry about anything."

Right. Look how that had gone so far.

He glanced in the rearview mirror as another pair of headlights grew bigger and brighter behind them.

"Sawyer... I think we have a tail," Everly said.

"I see them."

God, please let this not be a tail.

But even as the prayer exited his heart, he knew they were being followed. The vehicle behind them—a very large vehicle—was closing in.

He could hope they would get stuck or lose control in the weather. Sawyer accelerated and the tires spun out before gaining traction.

Don't hydroplane.

He pushed everything else out of his mind and focused on one thing: getting them out of this.

Getting them someplace safe.

"Can you call 911 and let them know we have a tail? Find out how long it will take for them to get to us? Tell them we're on Lost Trail Road heading north and need assistance immediately."

Everly got on her cell and made the call. He listened as she spoke into the phone, her voice conveying the urgency.

"What?" she asked. "Well, that's just great. What are we supposed to—" She huffed. "Hello? Hello? Are you still there? I lost the signal."

"What's happening? What got you upset?"

"The road is closed coming from the direction we're heading."

"Are you saying we're cut off completely?"

"That's what I'm saying. Someone needs to fix the roads out here if flooding can cut you off."

"If it was that easy, no one would ever be cut off."

"I'm going to call my brothers. See if we can get the helicopter to evacuate us. Except… I can't get a signal. What is going on?"

"Try mine. It's in the console."

Everly grabbed it. "No signal. Is this a dead zone or something?"

"I don't know. Maybe a cell tower is out."

Layla whimpered from the back seat. "What are we going to do?"

"I'm going to drive as long as I can and try to put distance between us and the monster vehicle behind us."

"'Monster vehicle?'" Layla asked.

"I'm thinking maybe a Hummer. I thought I saw one on the island earlier."

Everly glanced over her shoulder at the lights behind them. "We're losing them, at least for now."

"Maybe they weren't following us to begin with," Layla said. "Do you think that could be it—they aren't following us?"

"I don't know, honey, but we're getting out of here, regardless."

"I'm scared."

Sawyer would never admit it to her, but he was concerned too. *Okay, yeah, I'm scared.*

But Layla and maybe even Everly didn't need to hear that from him. Layla needed him to be strong. She needed Everly to be strong for her too.

Strong and smart.

"I hope your brother won't mind me taking this off the beaten path," he said.

"I don't think you have much choice." She reached for the handgrip again. "I think we're to the end of the road. At least I don't see the other vehicle's lights after that last curve in the road."

Yet.

Floodwaters raced across the way...*behind* a large tree that had fallen, blocking their path.

God, a little help, please?

He put the vehicle in Park and pounded the steering wheel. Everything he tried got thrown back in his face. Everly's hand squeezed his shoulder. "It's going to be okay."

Right. Everly was right. At least, he really wanted to *believe* she was right.

She was the strong one.

"What now?" Layla gasped, choking back a sob.

"She's hyperventilating." Everly hopped out and climbed into the back seat. "It's okay, Layla. Just calm down."

Sawyer surveyed the area surrounding the road. Someone's fenced-in property stood between him and freedom.

He backed up, then floored the accelerator. The tires slung mud, then gained traction. The vehicle raced forward and crashed right through the wooden fencing. Once through the fence, the tires spun out but once again gained traction. He accelerated across the beautiful green grass, tearing up the meadow. Maybe the property owners would understand their urgent need to escape once he explained that bad guys chased them.

But that was just it. He couldn't tell anyone anything more than he had already told Everly. Someone was trying to get to him. Trying to get to *Layla* to get to him. The vehicle slipped left; then he overcorrected and ended up doing doughnuts. He straightened out before flooring it again.

If they could just find a safe place to wait out the night. *God, please let us find that place.*

Or maybe they should have stayed at the house.

Doubts tortured him; then the vehicle lurched to the left and stopped, thrusting him forward. The seat belt kept him in place. He glanced behind him. "Everyone all right?"

"We're fine," Everly said.

He tried to free the vehicle, but no amount of accelerating or shifting gears would release the tires from the soggy ground.

"We're on foot now. We can do this." Everly tugged Layla's hood over her head. "Grab your backpack."

"Uncle Sawyer, are we going to have to run away in the storm?"

In her question, he felt all his failures culminating, drilling down into his bones.

Everly had already climbed out and was holding the door open for Layla, who clearly didn't like what they were facing. But Everly didn't like it either.

"Come on. Let's test out these Columbia raincoats made for the Pacific Northwest." She injected a teasing tone into her words, but it fell flat.

Way to go.

Sawyer shut his door on the other side. The wind had died down, but it could come raging back. The rain wasn't coming down in a torrent, but it was still coming down. In the distance, an engine rumbled.

The Hummer? Sawyer moved around the vehicle, and she saw the answer on his face.

"Let's go."

She heard the urgency in his words and suspected that he didn't want to scare Layla because having to take time to coddle her would do no one any good. She hooked her arm through Layla's, and together they followed Sawyer as he tromped through the muddy field.

"I'm cold," Layla said. "Aren't you cold?"

"Yes. But this will be over soon."

"When? When will it be over?"

"We're going to find a house where we can hide for the night." Why did she keep saying words she had no way of knowing were true? But she had to encourage Layla, whatever it took.

Everly couldn't imagine the people in the Hummer wouldn't find them eventually if they tried. Then again, if it was the same guys they'd tackled at the house, one of them needed medical attention—if he wasn't already dead.

Layla shivered next to her.

Lord, we're going to need some help, and fast.

They could all suffer from hypothermia if they had to stay outside on this cold, rainy night.

"I see something." Sawyer stopped in front of them. "It's a house. The lights are out except for the security light."

"So they still have electricity," she said.

The enticing thought of getting cozy in a warm house flooded her mind. At the moment, it was her greatest desire. She urged Layla forward, and they passed Sawyer, who hadn't moved.

"But what if we bring danger to them?" He still wasn't following them.

"If we don't stop at that house, they're still in danger. If we're being followed, the followers will stop at that house, looking for us whether we're there or not. Better to warn them. To call for help. Get a helicopter out here."

At least, that's how she justified making their way to the house. But were her thoughts out of desperation?

Yeah. Sure.

Everly could admit that she was desperate. "Unless you know about a cave we could huddle in and build a fire, the house is it."

Or the next house—but how far was that? She wasn't sure how much farther Layla could go in this cold. At the front door, she rang the doorbell but heard no activity inside. Then she pounded on the door.

When no one answered, she raised her voice: "My name is Everly Honor. Our vehicle got stuck. We need your help. If you won't open the door, can you please call a number for me?"

She looked at Sawyer.

He shrugged. "What if they're not home?"

"Look, if you're there, you'd better say something, and we'll move on. Because right now this is life or death, and we're coming inside if you're not home. So let us know if you are."

No answer. Sawyer hopped off the porch and then looked through a window. He moved over to the next window, then shook his head. "I think the house is empty. Wait here on the porch where it's dry, and I'll check the garage."

Everly pulled Layla to her, wrapped her arms around the girl to keep her warm and waited on Sawyer. She peered into the darkness. So far, the Hummer headlights hadn't come down this part of the road all the way, or else they might have easily seen the path they had carved across the field. The road was washing out in places. All she could think was the Hummer might have gotten stuck because those things were heavy and known for sinking in mud. Whatever delayed them, it was only temporary.

She almost wanted to pump her fist.

Footfalls sloshed through the grass and Sawyer appeared. He bounded up the steps. "No vehicle. They're gone. I feel just terrible about this, but we need help." He looked at her.

"Me? You want me to break in?"

"I thought you might have the skills."

"Why, because I'm security?"

"You were police. You know how to do things."

Yeah. Sawyer had been military. He hadn't told her, but she knew. Military before he'd had his import-export business.

"Do you even know your neighbors?" she asked.

"I…" He shrugged. "I don't know these particular neighbors."

"Are there others you know?"

"Yes, but they're in the other direction, and we can't go back that way. Layla needs to get out of this weather now."

He was right.

Everly tugged a tool kit out of her pack and quickly opened the door. She was glad Sawyer didn't ask more questions.

"They could have a silent alarm," she said, "but if someone shows up to check on the house, that will work for us. We need help."

Once inside, Layla reached for the lights.

"Don't!" Sawyer and Everly said at the same time.

"No lights," Sawyer said. "We don't want to draw attention if someone is still searching for us."

"Let me make sure the house is empty. Just wait right here." Everly moved closer to the steps. "Hello? Anyone home? We need help. I don't mean to intrude, but if you're here, please let us know. Can you help us? Call someone for us?"

When no one answered, she moved upstairs to clear the house, knowing that at any moment, she could get shot for trespassing. But she hoped her warnings would let the owners know they were no threat.

Once they settled in, Everly would try to reach her brothers and ask for that helicopter, but the weather could still prohibit them from getting here. The bedrooms were all empty, as were the bathrooms and closets. No one was hiding under the bed.

She went back downstairs and found Sawyer arranging logs in the fireplace.

"What are you doing?" she asked. "The smoke could give us away."

"Not in the storm. Not tonight."

"Just turn up the heat," she said.

"Layla wants a fire. I'm giving it to her."

And apparently, he needed to build one. Everly went into the kitchen and, using her flashlight, she found hot cocoa packets and made them drinks that would take the chill away.

Wrapped in a throw blanket, Layla had lain down on the sofa nearest the fire. Was she asleep already?

Everly set the mugs on coasters on the coffee table. A cozy fire crackled, giving off a little light in the house.

The adrenaline crashed right out of her, and she needed to… She wasn't sure what she needed to do.

Sawyer was at her side, pulling her to him. He pressed his face into her neck. Wholly inappropriate and yet completely natural. She slid her arms around him and let him hold her. She held him too. She had no emotional energy to resist the draw he had on her.

At least for this one moment in time, she would allow him to comfort her. She would comfort him in return.

Comforting wasn't technically part of her job, but she wasn't a robot. That aside, this was Sawyer. She had loved him. But then Sawyer had left her behind as if she had no value at all. Had meant nothing to him. Though his reasons were valid, Everly would never fall for someone so completely again.

She would never trust again.

And with that thought, she dropped her arms and stepped out of his grip.

"I need to call my brothers to come and get us." She'd been focused on securing the house and then found Layla and Sawyer near the fire and, yeah, had a momentary slip. In his arms, of course.

Now was the time to refocus on protecting Layla. And this man from her past, whether he wanted protection or not.

But her cell still had no bars. She was relieved to find the owners had a landline. So many people had done away with landlines; but times like these, she could appreciate old-fashioned ways. After the call to Ayden, she breathed a sigh of relief as she hung up the phone.

When she turned, Sawyer was standing too close to her in the dark kitchen.

She startled. *You scared me!* But she wouldn't tell him that. Bodyguards weren't supposed to get scared.

"They're going to try to send the helicopter, but it's touch and go in this weather," she said. Brett had been a pilot in the Coast Guard, so if anyone could get them, it was him. "They should be here within half an hour." *God, please let it be so.*

"And once they get us, where are they taking us?"

"For now, back to the HPS headquarters."

"I didn't agree to that."

Okay, now she would let him hear her frustration with him. "Where would you have them take us, Sawyer? We can't trust those men won't find us. We have to get out of here." She practically growled out the words.

"And go to some protection services *headquarters*? I don't want to put Layla through that trauma."

She ground out her whispered words through gritted teeth and thrust her finger into his chest. "Layla is already going through trauma. You've already put her through it."

She'd give anything if she could take back those last words. It wasn't her place to blame him for what was happening.

But was he to blame?

TWELVE

Sawyer took a step back. Everly's outburst surprised him. He realized his mouth was hanging open; he couldn't find the words to respond.

Everly had shown him what she really thought of him, and the pain of her words cut through his heart. Why did he care what she thought? He didn't know, but whatever the reason, he cared. And she'd hurt him. But the ache in his chest had as much to do with the truth of her words.

The very thing he'd tried to prevent—Layla going through a violent trauma—was happening.

Because of me.

The whole reason he'd hired a bodyguard was coming down on him like a self-fulfilling prophecy.

Before he could form a proper response, she whispered, "I'm sorry. I shouldn't have said that. I shouldn't have been so harsh."

"But you told me the truth as you see it."

She closed the gap he'd created when he'd stepped away. "It's not a truth as I see it, Sawyer. It's simply the facts. Look at what's happened tonight. But none of this is your fault, and I shouldn't have blamed you. Please...just forget I said it. I didn't mean it."

"You're right. I'm sorry to buck you at every turn. I

know you're only trying to protect her, but so am I. I thought you would have a safe house—as in, an actual place where Layla could at least be comfortable. Being displaced is hard enough, especially considering the cause."

"I understand. I had tried to arrange for one. It will be available in a few days. But in the meantime, our facilities are set up to accommodate guests in a comfortable way, I assure you."

She rubbed her arms and he realized she was still soaking wet. He wanted to wrap her in his arms again. They both shivered with the heating unit still turned down, so the house temperature was less than optimal.

But he wanted to wrap his arms around her for more than simply to share his warmth. He still cared deeply for Everly. And since he cared for her, he knew that he couldn't hurt her again, so he refused to let anything romantic happen between them.

"Let's get closer to the fire so you can warm up," he said. "It sounds like it could be a while before the helicopter arrives."

"During which time, I need to be on the lookout for anyone who tries to ambush us again like they did at your house. This place has no alarm system." Her face shifted to the ultimate professional protector, and she reached for her gun. "You hired me to protect Layla, and I'm asking you to let me do it." Anger still edged her tone. Everly went to look out the windows. "I'm going outside to check the perimeter."

He grabbed her wrist and swung her around. "Don't. Please just stay inside with me until help arrives. I don't want anything to happen to you. I can't be the reason you get hurt."

"What hurts me is that you don't trust me enough to

protect you." She shrugged free of his grip and chambered a round. "I'm good at what I do, Sawyer."

"I don't doubt that—and I *do* trust you, Everly." He leveled his gaze on her, willing her to feel the depth of his emotion and trust, though he realized that was a mistake. He shouldn't try to connect with her emotionally.

"Stay inside with Layla. I'll be right back."

She exited the kitchen, unlocked and opened the back door, and stepped out. The rain was a steady patter now, and the wind had calmed. That was good. The helicopter could come, but the bad guys could also be closing in on them.

He pressed his hands against his face and held back the deep, aching sob that tried to escape.

Lord, I never wanted Layla to go through this.

For all his efforts, he was the one to endanger his only living relative, his precious niece who meant everything to him, all because he tried to help others. And Everly— he'd endangered her by *asking* her to protect Layla.

He crept into the living room so he wouldn't wake Layla. The fire was dying out, and he stoked it quietly while trying to shove aside his concern for Everly. He should go outside with her and help hold down the fort, but she'd told him to stay inside. Going outside would only confirm to her that he didn't trust her.

He knew she was a professional and good at what she did, but skilled protection specialists got hurt too.

Sawyer looked at Layla. Her eyes were closed, but something about her told him that she wasn't asleep. She was only pretending to sleep. He couldn't blame her.

Lord, how do I protect her?

If he tried to disappear again—take Layla and just fall off the grid and into a new place to start over, to escape the madness—she wouldn't go for it.

Layla had friends and a life here.

And pulling her from that life could be more traumatic than the last twenty-four hours for a girl her age. Plus, Layla was plugged into social media. She would give up their location; so in the end, running and hiding would be for nothing. Layla was not someone he could trust in that arena. He didn't hold that against her. She was just a kid, after all.

The door opened and closed, and Everly rushed inside, soaking wet again. She was breathing hard too.

Layla sat up, wide awake. Like he had thought, she hadn't been asleep.

"What's happened?" he asked.

"The helicopter's coming. It's landing."

"That's great."

"That's not all. The others are coming too. The helicopter lights flashed across the field, and I saw them crossing the field on foot. They know we're about to escape, so they will rush toward the house now."

Fear spiked through him. Sawyer pulled Layla to her feet and handed her the backpack. "We have to hurry."

Everly nodded and held her gun at the ready as she opened the door. "On my signal, we make a run for it out the back door."

Gunfire shattered the windows.

"Now!"

Everly was relieved when the helicopter landed behind the house, but she continued running. Sawyer rushed Layla through the kitchen door, and they raced toward the waiting bird, the rotor wash whipping up the rain around them. The noise made it impossible to hear if the men were closing in.

But she already knew they were.

Protecting them, Everly held her gun at the ready, half running, half backing her way toward the helicopter. She'd seen two men crossing the field in front of the house. Their vehicle, left stuck in the meadow, had given them away. She couldn't be certain more hired guns weren't angling at them from other directions. Behind the house from the woods? From the side—again from the woods? Except for the wide meadow in front, trees closed in from all sides. She couldn't know how many more men there might be, but at least she'd taken one out with that shot to the leg. No way could he be one of the men running toward them.

A glance told her Sawyer and Layla were inside the helicopter. Good. They were safe now.

She continued moving toward the helicopter, facing the area where at least the men she knew of would approach. A couple of guys rushed around from the side of the house and fired.

"Everly, come on!"

A chorus of voices shouted from behind as she fired her gun to give them all cover.

If she turned to run, then she could be shot in the back. She continued stepping backward, firing her weapon. She could hear Layla scream from inside the helicopter.

The helicopter started lifting off.

I'm not going to make it.

Please just get them to safety, Brett. The men weren't after Everly, and she might need to stay behind to take them out. Or she could make a run for it and hide. They wouldn't waste their time on her.

Strong arms wrapped around her waist from behind.

"I got you!" Sawyer shouted as he held on to her.

"No. Get back inside the helicopter. Get out of here." But his grip only tightened as he lifted her off her feet and rushed her toward the helicopter while she fired more rounds toward the men, giving cover.

Once at the bird, Sawyer got her inside as she continued to lay down cover.

The helicopter lifted and tilted, and bullets pinged off the bottom. She buckled into the harness and donned the headphones. Her chest rose and fell as she gulped air and looked at the two sitting across from her, also wearing headphones.

"Is anyone hurt?"

"We're alive, thanks to you and your team," Sawyer said.

He held her gaze as if willing her to see the admiration in his eyes. She blew out a breath and closed her eyes.

"Thanks, Brett," she said. "You arrived in the nick of time."

"God's protection, Everly. I almost didn't make it. But you did a great job covering and protecting Sawyer and Layla."

"It was a team effort," she said. "We'll have to contact the homeowners and explain what took place. The police will need to investigate, so it's a crime scene as well. Maybe tomorrow we can try to repair the window so the storm won't create water damage."

That made two houses they needed to work on, thanks to these jerks.

"Relax, sis. You've got your hands full. We'll handle the house."

For the first time since she had started this assignment, she allowed herself to relax, if only a little. The hum and vibration of the helicopter soothed her nerves and, if she kept her eyes closed, she might actually fall asleep.

Would that be such a bad thing?

Yes. Yes, it would.

This was no time to relax. She needed to focus on others.

Poor Layla. She had to be scared to death.

Sawyer was traumatized as well, given what he and his niece had just gone through. Someone had shot at them. And now they couldn't go back home. They needed Everly now like never before.

She opened her eyes to find them both resting, eyes closed. Or sleeping? Nah, she doubted it. Maybe they had both followed her lead and closed their eyes.

Brett finally landed the helicopter on the roof of the obscure building where Honor Protection Specialists had made their headquarters. The chopper powered down, and Everly released her harness. Sawyer assisted Layla with hers.

Everly sat forward. "It's going to be okay. You'll be safe here until we find you another safe house, but we can all hope and pray these guys are captured in short order."

Everly hopped out of the helicopter first. Brett stood there, waiting.

"Anyone else here tonight?" she asked.

"Ayden and Caine are working, so it's just us."

She nodded, then turned to help Sawyer and Layla get out. "You got all your gear?"

Layla turned to show she still had her backpack. Sawyer lifted his duffel. Everly smiled. Hard to believe they had been on the run and still managed to hold on to a few things.

"Good. Follow me." She led them toward the entrance, through the door and down a flight of stairs. Brett pulled up the rear. No one could have followed them or known where they had gone.

Even if someone happened to know the HPS head-quarter address, which wasn't public knowledge, their facilities were locked down and safe. No one was getting in without an invitation. She would explain all this to Sawyer but didn't want to talk about it in front of Layla. Once inside, she ushered them down a long hallway to the area that held the guest rooms—a few rooms that served as a secure location in case another safe house wasn't available.

Like tonight.

Hotels were often used as safe houses by agencies such as the US Marshals service, but HPS preferred private homes or their own facilities.

A glance at Brett rewarded her with a wink, and he gestured toward one of the doors. She opened it wide to reveal a bed with a pink-and-purple comforter, along with fluffy pink pillows. A few age-appropriate posters, a comfy chair and a desk. Dresser and closet, and a small bathroom with a bath and shower. Everything someone would need to be comfortable for any length of stay, but on Everly's suggestion, Brett had made it special—just in case they ended up here.

"Layla, this is your room." Everly smiled.

Layla entered. Eyes wide, she sucked in a breath.

"Wait a minute," Sawyer said. "We need to stay together. Layla, you're with me."

"It's all right, Uncle Sawyer. This room is great, and I feel safe." She turned in a circle. "I'm okay. I can't sleep in the same room with you, anyway. You snore." She glanced at Everly. "You did this. Thank you, Everly."

Layla hugged her.

Her heart full, Everly pressed her cheek against the top of Layla's head. "You're very welcome."

I'm just sorry it came to this.

She released Layla, who quickly tossed her backpack on the bed. But Everly realized Sawyer hadn't given his approval, and ultimately the decision was up to him. She and Brett waited for his response.

He blew out a breath, and his shoulders sagged. "Does your cell work in here? You can text me if you need me."

"Um… I believe it would be prudent to keep your cell phones turned off," Everly said.

"What? Why?" Layla's eyes widened.

"She's right," Sawyer said. He tugged his out and turned it off, then handed it over to Everly. "Layla, let me see yours."

"I can turn it off myself." She lifted her chin.

He stuck his hand out, holding the palm flat. "I'll turn it off for you. Humor me."

She defiantly stared him down for a few moments. "Explain why."

"Someone could track you by your phone, that's why," Everly said. "Someone followed us. Someone shot at us. Your phone could lead them to us. Do you want that?"

Her shoulders slumped. "Of course I don't." She handed her cell to Sawyer and kept her hand out, as if expecting him to return it.

He powered it down, then handed both cells to Everly. "See? I'm giving my phone to Everly too. She can make sure we're not tracked that way."

"Because even though they are turned off, they can still emit signals if someone has the right equipment to look for them. We don't know who is after you. I'll put them in Faraday Bags."

"What's a Faraday Bag?" Layla asked.

"It's a container that's lined with a special combination of metallic materials that can shield devices from outside signals. Don't worry. You'll get them back as soon as this is over." Layla gave Everly and Sawyer a severe frown, then held the door open as if she was ready for them to leave. They all stepped out and she shut the door, almost in their faces.

"I apologize for my niece."

"No need. She's exhausted, as I'm sure you are." Brett opened the door directly across from Layla's room. "Maybe it wouldn't be a bad idea if you roomed together. This room has a bunk bed. But we can see how it goes."

"If there's a problem," Everly added, "we can rearrange things."

Sawyer stepped partially into the room. "Uh…where's the bathroom?"

Everly pushed by him and gestured to an open door that Sawyer had missed. He followed her inside.

"Each room has a bathroom that's fully outfitted with both bath and a shower."

"Wow. You guys have thought of everything."

Everly left the room and hovered in the open door.

"We try." Brett was backing his way down the hall. "I'll be here all night along with Everly. You guys need anything, I'm in the last office to the left."

"I can't thank you enough, Everly. You saved our lives."

"As mentioned before, it was a team effort." She couldn't tear her gaze away and, of course, that moment he'd pulled her to him and pressed his face against her neck—that vulnerable moment—came rushing back to her.

Time to get out of here. "Well, get some rest. We have a lot to talk about, but later. For tonight, you're safe. Sleep well."

"I hope that you'll rest, too, since we're finally here. You can show me around tomorrow."

"Sounds good."

Sawyer started closing the door.

"Sawyer, wait."

He opened it wide again and waited expectantly.

"Maybe you'll tell me the rest of the story soon."

"Yeah. Maybe I will."

THIRTEEN

Sawyer was too exhausted to sleep. Did that make any sense? He didn't know but was too tired to figure it out.

Something gnawed at the back of his mind.

Wonder if they'd mind if I explore?

They probably didn't want people roaming around without an escort. Likely had cameras everywhere. He just wanted coffee. Well, not really, but that would be his excuse for roaming the halls. Still, he could smell it brewing and followed the aroma to the bright white kitchen, expecting to find...

Everly's back was to him as she poured herself a cup.

A Bible scripture took up half the wall in flowing script: *Do not be afraid; only believe. Mark 5:36*

The words jumped out at him as if they were meant precisely for him at this moment in time.

I'm trying, Lord, I'm trying.

While that surprised him, he found it comforting.

Everly turned around, her brows arching when she saw him. Her hair was disheveled. He wanted to run his fingers through it.

Really?

He stepped all the way into the kitchen. "I didn't mean to surprise you."

"You weren't able to sleep either?" She took a sip from her mug.

"No... I..." Where should he begin?

She smiled and held up the cup. "You want some coffee?"

"No, because I'm *planning* on getting to sleep. But there was something I needed to do first."

That gnawing at the back of his mind... He was wrapping his head around it now.

"I get it. You want your cell phone back. I'll get you a burner to use while you're here."

"Not that. Um..."

"Why don't we talk with a view?"

"Huh?"

"Follow me."

He followed Everly down a hall and through a gym to a large expanse of a room with covered windows for a wall on one side. With the touch of a button, the blinds slowly opened.

The view took his breath away. "The sky cleared enough to see. Wow."

Everly stood near the window. "It never gets old. Another storm will come through, but for a few minutes, we can see the moonlight shining on Mt. Rainier."

"It's...beautiful," he said. *Just like you.*

She gestured to a sofa.

He eased into it.

"You sought me out for a reason," she said.

Had he sought her out? Yeah...that was it.

"I did." Except he might be losing his nerve now.

"Well, here I am."

"I'm sorry... Just..."

"You're chickening out, aren't you?"

"What? No. How did you—"

"You can trust me, Sawyer. Don't you know that by now?"

He hung his head. "I've always known it."

When he lifted his head, she was looking at the view and he joined her—only his view had silky brown hair and hazel eyes. A pert little nose, sculpted cheeks and supple pink lips.

Get over her.

He drew in a long breath. He needed to get this over with. Once and for all.

"After Paisley died and I moved back to the States to raise Layla, I knew I had to do something. I had to make a difference."

He gulped a few breaths to calm his pounding heart.

I really am going to do this.

"I learned that Paisley had tried to get help. She didn't tell me because she didn't want me to give up my job and my life and come back for her. But she reached out to others locally. And…they all failed her."

"I'm so, so sorry. If I had known maybe…"

He held her gaze. "Look… I know you've been through something similar, Everly. I saw it in your eyes when I first told you about Paisley. I can see it in your eyes now. Did you have a stalker? Or were you abused?"

She blinked as if shocked at his words. "I…" Everly looked at the floor. Looked away from him. "You're right. I was stalked years ago. But…"

"I want to hear more about that. But only when you're ready. Okay?"

She finally lifted her gaze then breathed in deeply.

"Sure. I'll tell you everything. Anything you want to know. But later. I want to hear the rest of your story. What else, Sawyer? How did *you* try to help others?"

"My import/export consulting business. I use it as a

cover to assist women like Paisley who need help getting away from their abusers. I work with the local women's shelters and similar organizations to assist them into a new life where they won't be found. Where they'll be safe. I teach them how to stay safe."

And that's why this situation is driving me crazy.

Everly leaned forward, elbows on thighs. "Are you saying you give them a new identity?"

"They keep their names, in most cases, but a move to a new location in a new life is often enough to lose their predators and abusers."

"And the police?"

"Their hands are usually tied. Not much is done to protect someone who is being stalked or threatened with abuse. Restraining orders have their limitations. Believe me, I know. My sister had a restraining order against her ex-husband. That didn't prevent him from killing her."

"And that's why you don't want to tell the police? You think they can't help?"

"That isn't why. The reason is that my clients must have privacy. The more people who know, the greater the chances are their new life will be uncovered. Police keep reports, which are open to the public. There is… another reason."

"And what's that?"

"Two of the women I helped hide were married to law enforcement officers. Again, the fewer people who know, the safer the women will be. Plus, keeping private the information about myself and what I do, also protects them." He'd done it. He'd told her. Now he wondered why he'd waited so long. Still, with her connections to the police, he almost felt like he was betraying a trust.

Everly stood and moved to the window.

He followed her, hoping she would finally understand.

"I've told you about my life now, and I'm trusting you to keep it private. Keep it between us. Don't even share with your brothers. Everly, do you get it now?"

More than anything, he wanted her to get him, and to not believe he was the bad guy for being less than enthusiastic about having the police investigate.

When she pulled her attention from the view—the clouds once again covered the sky—her eyes shimmered in the dim lighting of the room.

She stepped closer. "I understand." She lifted her chin and ever so slowly leaned forward and pressed her lips against his.

She'd moved gradually, giving him a chance to step away, but he'd stood still, wanting this more than anything in the world. Sensations flooded his heart and mind, and he couldn't resist her anymore. He drew her into his arms and kissed her thoroughly until they were both breathless.

He hadn't wanted her to know how he felt inside. He hadn't even known how completely lost he was on her until this moment. Now he had made a huge mistake.

She stepped away and covered her mouth as if surprised at her own actions. Startled at what happened between them.

"I'm sorry," she said. "What you told me—I couldn't admire you more, Sawyer. I can't believe that I was ever suspicious of you. I thought you were keeping a heinous secret."

Ouch. That hurt. "Really?"

"Well, not really, but I was worried. Until you came clean, how could I know? You've been helping people and doing something good in this world, putting yourself at risk for others. I…I appreciate that in a visceral way."

"Since you had a stalker."

"Yes. I completely understand. I had to make a lot of

changes in my life to deal with that. Still… I shouldn't have kissed you."

Now was the moment of truth.

They wanted the kiss. They had each followed through with the kiss. But what next? With the look in her eyes, he dreaded her next words, but he would have his say first.

"It's okay. I kissed you back."

She sighed and put more distance between them.

"We both know that we can't have anything between us, right?" She angled her head, and her hair fell partially across her face.

"Right. I know." The moment he started questioning his own resolve to not let anything happen because he couldn't hurt either of them again, Everly made it clear she had her own reasons for avoiding a relationship with him. He could only guess at her reasons, but he suspected they were not far from his own.

He stared out into the darkness while she pressed the button, and together they watched the blinds close until there was nothing left to look at.

A girl's scream broke the silence. Sawyer raced toward the sound.

Everly ran after Sawyer, who made it to Layla's room first. But the door was locked. "Layla, honey, open the door." He sent a panicked glare at Everly. His gentle knock morphed into banging. "Layla, are you okay? Let me in!"

"Calm down," Everly said. "You're going to scare her."

Weapon drawn, Brett hurried toward them.

"We don't need a gun," Everly said. "We need a key."

"Oh. Right." Brett dug in his pocket, then pulled one out. "The master key."

He thrust it into the lock, then Sawyer slowly opened the door. "Layla... Honey..."

Lord, please let her be okay. It was probably just a dream.

Layla sat up in the bed, her face in her hands sobbing. Sawyer rushed to her. Everly's heart went out to them both.

"Let's give them privacy," she whispered to Brett as she started to close the door.

"Everly, wait," Layla said, choking back her tears. "Can you stay?"

Layla gave Sawyer an apologetic look and, although he appeared momentarily surprised—even hurt—he backed away.

"Sure." Everly sat on the edge of the bed and hugged Layla to her, then sent him an apologetic look too. She hadn't expected to see gratitude in his gaze.

She focused on Layla, and Sawyer left the room and closed the door.

"It's going to be okay. It was just a bad dream." Like she'd thought. Or was it something else?

She rubbed the girl's back to soothe her. "You've been through a lot, so it's understandable."

Finally, Layla's shoulders stopped shaking.

"You want to talk about it?"

Layla shifted away from her and shook her head. "There's nothing to talk about. Like you said, it was a bad dream."

"Do you think you can go back to sleep?"

"I don't know."

"What if I stay here with you until you fall asleep?"

"Maybe, but what if I just have another bad dream?"

"I'll tell you what—I'll get a cot moved in here, and I'll sleep with you." The door pushed open and Sawyer entered.

"You guys move to the room I'm in. There are cots already set up. I'll sleep in here." He shrugged and gave her a sheepish grin.

She didn't blame him for listening in on their conversation. In his position, she would have wanted to hear the conversation too. Even if Sawyer had been the one to comfort her, Everly wasn't so sure she wouldn't have been eavesdropping just to make sure all was well and no covert plans were being made to escape the facility.

"That's a great idea. Come on, Layla. Let's cross the hall. I'll sleep in the same room with you and wake you up if you start having a bad dream." Layla nodded and climbed out of bed.

In her purple sweats and white T-shirt, she followed Everly across the hall. Everly glanced behind her before she closed the door, and Sawyer sent her a silent thank-you.

After Layla was settled into the cot on the top, Everly took the bottom bunk and stared at the bed above her. She wasn't likely to fall asleep, considering that she'd promised to wake Layla, but her mind was filled with thoughts of all that Sawyer had shared about what he was up to.

She couldn't have imagined.

But she should have guessed. Sawyer was a good man, and she never should have doubted that; but so much bad had happened in his life that she couldn't have been sure that he wasn't up to illicit activities. And now, to learn that he *helped* people, helped women who were trying to escape their stalkers and abusers?

Warmth buzzed through her chest at the thought of him.

The victims' need for support was something she could appreciate more than most people. More than her brothers—they didn't even know she'd endured a stalker. She hadn't wanted them to know because it would change the way they looked at her and thought of her. Maybe. Or maybe not. But she wouldn't risk it. She'd taken care of the trouble on her own. After gaining the defensive skills she needed, she'd faced off with him. Turned the tables on him. Threatened him until he was scared of her. He disappeared, and she hadn't seen him again. She had no idea if she ever would because it had been seven years now, but she was prepared for anything.

Regardless, she understood why Sawyer hadn't wanted to share the information.

Now that she was armed with this new intel, Everly could look at who was after him from a different angle. Knowledge was power, as the saying went. Someone had the resources to hire men to invade his home. She wasn't certain if they planned to kill him or simply take him, but their approach had been haphazard at best. Whatever their goal, they were putting Sawyer's and Layla's lives at risk, and Everly's too.

Now that they were holed up at HPS headquarters, she itched to get to the computers so she could do some real work. While she liked the action of being in the field, her prowess lay in cyberspace.

Shifting to her side, she wished she could escape the room and work if she couldn't sleep, but she wouldn't lose Layla's trust. The decision made to go digital with her investigation tomorrow, she pushed those thoughts aside. Maybe now she could get some sleep.

But unfortunately, thoughts of the kiss she'd shared with Sawyer took their place.

I kissed him.

Had she truly freed herself from responsibility with her bold statement…

We both know that we can't have anything between us, right?

What had she been thinking, to cross that professional line?

But she hadn't been able to stop herself. The man was gorgeous—and to make matters worse, he was every woman's hero. All of that worked together, conspiring against her willpower, drawing her in toward him, and she'd taken that one step forward. Closer, until she smelled his musky scent.

Then…she couldn't have stopped herself from pressing her lips against his.

And the thing was—he'd kissed her back.

Thoroughly. Perfectly.

At the memory, her heart pounded.

Her lips tingled. She pressed her finger against them and closed her eyes.

Oh, Lord, what am I going to do?

FOURTEEN

Sawyer sat on the bed covered with the pink quilt that Everly had thoughtfully secured ahead of time. She couldn't have known they would end up here, and he'd fought to keep that from happening. But on the off chance they would have to come here for even one night, she'd arranged for the purchases to make Layla comfortable.

The woman was competent. Thoughtful. Sensitive. Beautiful.

To think he'd let her go all those years ago. To think he planned to let her go again.

He lay down and rested his head against the pillow and tugged the pink comforter over him.

His heart could be full. Could be happy in this moment in time. Layla trusted Everly, a woman he had once loved and obviously still cared deeply about. She was safe and secure in the other room.

And maybe he could actually get some sleep in what felt like a fortress.

Now that he had a few moments to rest, he closed his eyes, but images of kissing Everly immediately bombarded him. He remembered the feel of her and the smell of her and her soft lips, gentle and eager at the same moment. Kissing her now was nothing like when he had kissed her years before. They had both been through so much and were changed. Perhaps now, they each knew better what they wanted.

And what they *didn't* want.

She'd made that clear with her *"we can't have anything between us"* comment. He couldn't agree more, except that he'd been perfectly fine as a bachelor focused on helping others and taking care of his niece, until Everly's sudden appearance in his life for all the wrong reasons. The kiss had awakened things inside him better left to slumber.

Now what am I supposed to do?

And he'd shared his true self with her—the truth about what he was doing in his business. She was the one person outside of his clients and the very few in assistive organizations who knew.

Why had he shared?

It tied him to her in ways he wasn't sure he wanted. What if she let the truth slip to one of her police officer friends?

Sawyer tossed and turned, and finally, he smelled coffee. Time to get up. His first inclination was to check his cell phone, but he had turned it over to Everly. The room had no clock. Scraping a hand through his hair, he opened the door and stepped out into the hallway. Hovering at the door across the hall, he lifted his hand.

Should I? Or shouldn't I? It might be too early to wake Layla. And Everly should rest while she could. His things were still inside the room, so he couldn't grab them and take a shower.

Laughter drifted to him from down the corridor.

Layla was already up. He smiled; it had been a long time since he felt carefree, but he knew this emotion wouldn't last. They had work to do.

In the kitchen he found Layla at the table, eating eggs, bacon, toast, grapefruit and a doughnut on the side.

She smiled up at him. "It's about time you got up."

That's what he always said to her. He chuckled and sat at the table. "This might be the first time you beat me. What time is it anyway?

He glanced at the clock as he asked the question. Almost 7:30 a.m. He never slept so late, but still felt like he hadn't slept at all.

Brett stuck a plate in front of him.

"Where's Everly?" Sawyer asked.

"She's working. She told me to let you sleep." Layla took a bite of toast.

She appeared bright-eyed and rested, even after the terrible day they had yesterday.

"Did somebody say my name?" Everly walked around him to the coffeepot.

She looked at his face, and a V formed between her brows. "Did you sleep at all?"

"That bad, huh?"

She gave a subtle nod. "Eat up. Get ready. We have work to do."

"What did you have in mind?"

Brett thrust a big mug of coffee at him. "Eat and drink first. Talk later."

Every leaned against the counter after filling her own mug, and from behind Layla, she gave him a look.

Maybe he *did* need coffee because it took him a few moments to assess that look.

Duh. She didn't want to talk in front of Layla.

"Everly says I'm not going to school today, and you need to call in an excuse. I already took yesterday off with you two and see where it got me. If I'm going to miss, I need my work to do at home so I don't get behind."

He glanced up at Everly, not at all happy that she had made that decision without him. Before he could respond, Everly spoke.

"It's your call, Sawyer, but I think we need to do threat analysis and assess everything. Maybe tomorrow she can go back. But again, you decide. She asked about school, and I told her I didn't think it was a good idea today. But I also said that her uncle had the final say."

What was he thinking? "I'll contact the school and see about getting your work." He took a long swig of black coffee.

He was going to need a lot of it today.

After Sawyer showered and dressed, he found Everly in a room with multiple computers and monitors. "Where's Layla?"

"Brett is keeping her occupied. I think they're playing Zelda right now. We have a basketball court too. Did you know she likes basketball?"

The news surprised him. "I... Uh...no." He should know more about his own niece.

Everly stared at one of the computer screens. He suspected that she hadn't meant her comment in a condescending way—more that she was surprised to learn the news.

"So maybe we can play later," Sawyer said. "You and Brett against me and Layla."

She pulled her gaze from the screen. "That's the plan. But it depends on how the day goes. Come sit next to me. I have a few things to show you."

He eased into the swivel office chair she'd placed next to her. "Everly, you know I only hired you to protect Layla. You're going above and beyond duty here. I...I'll pay you for whatever you do, of course."

Her expression turned serious. "Not to worry."

He wasn't sure how he felt about it.

"Please, Sawyer. Don't waste your energy worrying about money. What's important is that we find out who is after you and what is going on." Everly faced the computer screen again and brought up images.

"Looks like you've been busy this morning."

"Yes. I've gained permission to access video footage from cameras surrounding the accident you were in with the truck. It's a fuzzy shot and a bad angle, but do you see him?"

"Yeah. Is that the person you said acted suspicious?"

"Yes. Watch the video and see what you think."

"I can't really see his face."

"I'll have to work on that so maybe we can get a good-enough image to utilize facial-recognition software."

He was taken aback by her statement. HPS had those kinds of capabilities? Admittedly, he hadn't done much research on the organization; because he knew Everly, personally, he'd wanted her as a bodyguard for Layla.

He grew more impressed with her, and with HPS, by the moment.

And weirdly, it was also unfortunate that Layla grew more impressed with her. Because at the end of this drama, he and Everly would part ways. He saw now that parting ways could very well break Layla's heart.

Sawyer had resolved he wouldn't break his or Everly's heart, and now Layla's was on the line as well.

Lord, why is every decision so hard?

"Earth to Sawyer... Hello, McFly." Everly stared at him. He finally focused in on her.

"Where were you?" She shook her head and returned her attention to the monitor. "Don't answer that. It's been a hard few days, and I'm sure it's difficult to focus on just one thing."

He cleared his throat. "Thank you for understanding."

Honestly, she'd gotten the weird feeling that he was thinking about her. About...*them*.

She let the video play again. "So, do you see what I'm talking about?" *Or am I just so completely paranoid, given my past stalker issues, that everyone is a stalker?*

"I think you're right. He seems to zero in on the intersection, then steps forward as if expecting something to happen."

Sawyer flinched next to her as if remembering the impact of the crash, even though no sound came through the feed.

"Are you okay?" she asked.

He had been a rock through this crisis, but still, she worried about his mental state.

"I'll be better when we figure this out."

"We will, Sawyer. We will."

"Like that scripture on the wall in the kitchen. 'Do not be afraid; only believe.'"

Her faith had grown since she'd known Sawyer before, and her heart jumped at his words. "Yes. We need to have faith and trust God that He'll see us through this."

He nodded. "So what do we do with this information?"

"I'll send this over to an expert who can hopefully clean this up so we can get a face and his identity, as I mentioned. In the meantime, I say we track down the truck driver."

"I tried that, remember?"

"You didn't try it with my help."

"Actually, I did. You gave me the contact information." He grinned.

She loved that grin. "That's fair. But I have another idea. This guy, Kevin Ellis, is key to what's going on."

"What about the Cadillac license plate number? Have we learned anything?"

"Detective Mann will let us know. He's working on that, I'm sure."

"Then what's your idea?"

"When people run and hide, where do they go?" His response would be interesting, considering he made it his business to help people do just that. And the thought of the sacrifices he made to help others made her heart glad when she didn't want one more reason to be drawn closer to him.

He shrugged and stared at her.

"Since you help people, you probably already know that they will go to—"

"Friends or family."

"Exactly. Someone they know or trust. But you also know…"

"They can be found." He nodded. "I see where you're going with this."

Finally. Sawyer might have woken up. His eyes looked a little brighter. He glanced at the coffee mug he'd brought with him. "You found someone, someplace where we can look for him."

She grinned and nodded. "I did. He has a cousin in the next town over."

"You think he'd be that dim-witted to believe someone wouldn't track him there?"

"No. But his cousin knows where he is."

Sawyer studied her, then his eyes narrowed. "You didn't."

"Caine had a couple of days between assignments, so he watched the cousin's house and followed him."

Sawyer sat up taller. "Don't leave me hanging."

"The cousin bumped into a guy downtown and passed off a sack. I'm assuming it held cash. Ellis will not want to visit an ATM or use credit cards. At least he's that smart."

"And apparently that scared."

"Exactly. Then Caine followed the guy with the sack to a motel just outside of town. He hasn't left the room. So we need to hurry."

"You're sure this guy is Ellis?"

"He changed his appearance a bit. Shaved his head and wears a cap. Put on some glasses. But it's him."

"So you told your detective friend?"

"Yes. I needed to find out if the investigation into the car accident is still open. Detective Mann has invited me to pursue this lead." Especially since Lincoln knew that Sawyer would reveal more working with her, since he hired her. But she hoped that Sawyer wasn't upset with her. "I understand why you avoid getting the police involved, Sawyer. But we need to do this aboveboard and the right way."

"Or you could lose your license." He frowned.

"Yes, but we also want any of our discoveries to be used in court if a charge is brought. We don't want a criminal to go free on a technicality."

She leaned closer and rested her hand on his shoulder. "I worked with Lincoln before when I was a cop, and I've worked with him while at HPS. He can be trusted."

"But the information will be available to the public. Or to other officers."

"Right now, that's the least of your worries. Someone has come close to taking you—and Layla—down. Now, let's go question this guy."

"What about your cop friend?"

"He was intrigued to learn that I found Ellis. Again, he invited me into this active investigation because right now, this is the fastest way for us to get answers. Your lives are in danger. Kevin Ellis's life is also in danger. Lincoln trusts me to handle this professionally, and he'll be nearby to bring Ellis in."

"His actions say that he's guilty."

"I think we both know that actions don't always reveal the true picture. He's scared, though. That much is obvious."

Sawyer blew out a breath—a distinctively pleasant sigh. "I have to tell you, Everly... I'm impressed."

"What? You didn't think we could do it?"

"I don't really know what I was thinking."

"With everything that's happened, it's to be expected."

"Is there anything else you've learned—" he cleared his throat "—while I was sleeping?"

She chuckled and stood. "Nothing concrete yet. We talk to this guy, and then we get answers."

Sawyer stood. "You said 'we.' What about Layla? We can't just leave her here."

"Come on." She gestured to him, and he followed her out of the room and down the long hallway.

She heard the typical sounds of shoes squeaking on a gym floor. At the wide-open doors, they stood and watched Brett and Layla shooting hoops.

"I think she's made a new friend." Everly crossed her arms.

"I don't know. I mean..."

"You hired a male bodyguard before me and had no issues leaving her with him."

"I guess you're right."

"There's no guessing about it."

At least today, Layla was safe and secure here.

Layla shouted with joy after she made a basket, then spotted Sawyer and ran over. "Uncle Sawyer, did you come to play?"

His smile was filled with love. "When I get back, I'll challenge you."

"Where are you going?"

"I have to take care of some business, but we shouldn't be too long."

"'We'?" Layla glanced between Sawyer and Everly. "You're going too?" Her shoulders slumped. "Do I have to go?"

"If you go with us, you'll just have to sit in the car."

"Forget that. I'd rather stay here. Can I stay?" She looked at Sawyer.

"Of course you can."

"Awesome." She turned and dribbled the basketball toward Brett in a threatening back-and-forth fashion; then he blocked her. She laughed wildly.

Everly led Sawyer away from the gym, letting those images sink in for now.

Finally, he caught her arm and stopped her. "I had no idea. I mean… I thought I was raising her, but I feel like I don't even know her."

Yeah. She wasn't going to bring up that she had a few suspicions about Layla's texting activities to him again. She couldn't know for sure that Layla was texting with people who were probably outside of Sawyer's comfort zone. Everly could be overly suspicious, but Layla seemed secretive.

"Nobody knows everything about their kids. Again, give yourself a break. You've been a solid and loving person in her life. A father figure when she had no one."

He looked at her long and hard, longer than necessary,

and she wished he would stop. Then again, she held on to that look with everything in her.

"I can't thank you enough for what you've done. What you're doing. I don't know how Layla is going to let go of you after this is over and we say goodbye."

A knot lodged in her throat as she walked forward. Sawyer followed her toward the exit to the parking garage where they would take the rental SUV Ayden had secured for them. Her car was getting repaired, and Ayden's SUV was still being retrieved from the meadow on Blue Island where they left it last night. Sawyer's words still echoed in her thoughts. She'd been the one to set the boundaries, but hearing the words of finality from him felt like the old wound had ripped open.

FIFTEEN

Across the street from the motel, Sawyer started to get out.

"Wait here." Everly hopped out without waiting for his reply and jogged over to Caine's red Dodge Charger. She climbed in.

Sawyer rubbed his head. What were they saying? How long was this going to take? A few moments later, Everly got out, strode back and got into the vehicle.

"You could have just called him," Sawyer said.

"True, but in-person conversations can reveal more."

"You need the element of surprise with your own brother?"

She grinned. "My main concern is that someone else could have followed Ellis. Caine has been watching out for that possibility too. No one has found him. We need to talk to him now, get information out of him and then potentially see about securing his safety."

Sawyer's heart pounded too fast for comfort. His import-export endeavors held a degree of cloak-and-dagger, but nothing on this level. His chest ached at the fact that anyone ever had to run and hide in fear for their lives.

He drummed his fingers on the dash. "So what's the plan of approach?"

"We tell him who we are and that we need to know what happened. The truth is always best. He'll know if we're lying, and then he'll just clam up."

"Since he's hiding, he could clam up anyway."

"True enough. Let's go."

They got out and crossed the street. Sawyer walked next to Everly, letting her take the lead as they rounded the side of the hotel.

"Just relax. Act like we've booked a room and this is just another day."

"Easy enough for you to say."

"No. Not really."

Yes. Really. When she stopped in front of the door Caine had seen Ellis enter, moisture spread over Sawyer's palms. *I'm about to get answers. Then again, maybe not.*

God, please let me find out who is behind this.

Everly looked at Sawyer, then knocked on the door.

No one answered. Sawyer stiffened. *He's not going to talk to us.*

"Mr. Ellis, we need to talk. I'm Everly Honor with Honor Protection Specialists. I'm here with Sawyer Blackwood, the man whose vehicle you obliterated with your truck. We simply want to find who is behind this. You're not in trouble. We're not going to hurt you. And if you want your life back, I can help. Please open the door and let us in."

Sawyer waited a few breaths. Hoped and prayed.

Seconds ticked by. Everly lifted her hand to knock again, but Ellis spoke from the other side of the door.

"How do I know you are who you say you are?"

"If you look through the peephole, you'll see Mr. Blackwood. I'm sure you must recognize him."

Next to her, Sawyer tensed. Was the man going to open

the door and shoot them? Everly pressed her hand over her gun and slowly pulled it out.

Considering Ellis had rammed into Sawyer with his truck, they should be ready for anything.

He held his breath; then the dead bolt finally unlocked. The door swung open a few feet, and Kevin Ellis stared at them, his eyes narrowed. Was he trying to put on a strong front?

"Look, man, what do you want from me?" The man eyed Everly.

"We just want to ask a few questions," she said. "Standing outside your door could draw unwanted attention."

Ellis quickly ushered them in. Fast-food remnants were scattered on a small table. Empty cups and garbage on every flat surface.

"Excuse the mess."

Everly gestured to one of two chairs. "Why don't you have a seat?"

"I like standing. How did you find me?"

Everly crossed her arms. "That's the thing. It wasn't that hard. You're hiding for a reason, Mr. Ellis, and that is also not hard to figure out." Everly turned to Sawyer, and Ellis followed her gaze.

He took in Sawyer's face, his eyes lingering on the remaining bruise on his temple.

He held his hands up, palms out. "I was told nobody would die. And you're still alive."

Sawyer had thought he wanted to hear this man admit to treachery, but now acid rose in his throat. "Really? I almost died. I could have been burned alive in the car. Everly pulled me out."

"When I saw the fire, I got scared. The cops arrived, and I told them I didn't see you. My company was going to let me go after that. Your insurance company would probably sue them. Anyway, I wasn't sure what to do, but when I spotted someone following me, I knew I had to disappear."

Everly sent Sawyer a silencing look. She wanted to ask the questions. *Whatever.* He pushed the rising anger down—to a point.

"Go ahead and have a seat." Everly sat.

Get him to relax and he might talk more, although, he'd started talking pretty quickly.

Ellis sat on the edge of the bed, knocking off an empty Burger King sack. Sawyer took the remaining chair.

"So…you were told nobody would die," Everly said. "Who told you this, and what were you asked to do?"

Ellis's hands shook, and he gripped the chair. A bead of sweat trickled down his temple.

"I don't think I'll tell you anything more. I want a lawyer."

"We're not the police," Everly pressed. "Look at Mr. Blackwood. You almost killed him, and now someone has targeted his niece as well."

Don't forget yourself, Everly. He almost shivered at the thought of how many times they had almost been killed.

"If you don't tell us who hired you and someone dies, you could be held responsible," she said.

Was that true? Maybe she was exaggerating; but by the look on the man's face, her statement had the desired effect.

"I was told to make it look like an accident. That no one would die but just to shove the car off the road. I didn't know it would catch on fire. I'm sorry."

"How did you know I would even be at that intersection?" Sawyer didn't care that Everly sent him another silencing look.

"I don't know those details. I was told to park and then start moving forward at a very specific time and pace."

Had the Cadillac driver directed the truck driver? He'd been at the cemetery for a few moments, which had obviously given them enough time to try to coordinate this charade.

"People die in car accidents." Everly shook her head as if trying to grasp the stupidity. "Especially when a truck plows into them. What could make you do that? The only thing I can figure is that someone must have paid you."

He nodded. "Yes. They paid me a lot of money. I was broke before. My wife divorced me and took every penny. I…I don't have good insurance through my company and had a ton of medical bills with an autoimmune disorder. I said no at first, but then… I got so far behind on bills I thought I would never catch up. So I said yes. I made a mistake. I know that now. Look, I'm sorry—I made such a terrible decision. I would rather have money troubles than this."

"Why are you hiding now since you did as you were told? You knew you committed a crime, and you're running from the police?"

"No." He thrust his wrists out. "Cuff me now. I wish you *were* the police. Someone has been following me. The truth is, I'm afraid for my life now."

Everly released a slow sigh. "Because you can identify who hired you."

"That's why it doesn't make any sense. I can't identify anyone. It was all done over a text. Money was put into my bank account, but I'm afraid to access it now. Why does money matter if you're dead?"

Sawyer leaned forward. "Tell us about your divorce."

The man's eyes widened. "Why would you want to know about that? What does it have to do with this?"

Everly eyed him, too, her mouth twisting and pursing. "Just humor me. Who is her lawyer?"

"Some high-powered dude in Chicago."

That news sent a ping through him.

"Mr. Ellis," Everly said, "you drive a truck for a living, and your average salary with Kaycee Transport is below fifty thousand a year. How could your wife afford an influential lawyer from Chicago?"

"It wasn't her money. It was the man she left me for. She's incredibly beautiful. If you saw her you would understand why she is with the new guy. I don't know how or why she married me. But it's over, and now I've wrecked my life." He hung his head and coughed out what sounded like a sob.

Had he intended the pun? Probably not. The guy sobbed into his hands.

Everly texted someone.

Detective Mann?

"I tell you what, Mr. Ellis," she said. "You're scared and we're going to put you in protective custody. You don't have to run anymore. You only need to cooperate with the police."

He dropped his hands. "You called the cops on me?"

"I've informed my detective friend that you're willing to cooperate, but you want protection. What do you say?"

He sagged in the chair, defeated.

Sawyer could almost feel sorry for him. Almost.

The window shattered as gunfire exploded.

"Get down!"

Ellis dropped to the floor, and Sawyer covered him.

"You led them here," he shouted. "They're going to kill me now. They're going to kill all of us now!"

"Quiet!" Everly carefully peered out the side of the curtains.

They were trapped in the room. She got on her cell and dialed 911 to report shots were fired, then called Lincoln. He didn't answer. Worry for him shot through her. He could be out there, watching, and in the process of trying to nail down their shooter. Or...he could be incapacitated.

"I have to get out of here." Ellis shoved Sawyer away.

Holding her gun at the ready, Everly pressed her back against the wall and stared him down. "You'll die if you don't follow my instructions."

More gunfire cracked the windows, which were now riddled with bullet holes.

"Shoot them back," the man said. "What are you waiting for?"

Everly didn't answer. She couldn't see the shooter, and she couldn't randomly fire her gun into a parking lot. An innocent victim could get hurt or killed. Hopefully, the sound of gunfire had sent people into hiding in a secure location. The adrenaline rush reminded her of when she was a cop with the Tacoma PD.

She missed it...

But the rules for a protection service were only slightly different. The pressure was on her to make the right judgment call. She could lay down cover and provide a way for them to escape this room. Or they could wait.

Caine had left as soon as Everly and Sawyer approached, so he couldn't help.

Lord, what do I do in this predicament?

"I need your cell phone," Sawyer said. "I want to call and make sure Layla is okay."

She had never given him that burner phone she'd mentioned, so she tossed her cell to him. Sirens rang out, and

Everly let that knowledge bolster her. Maybe the approaching cops would scare the shooter away.

Then again, capturing the shooter would be the best scenario for them all. Ellis truly might not know who had paid him to harm Sawyer, and they needed answers. She gripped her gun and remained prepared to defend. But she would not take the next step and go on the offensive.

She peered out the window again but couldn't see the police cruisers yet. Nor any sign of Lincoln. Concern for her friend, as well as those in this motel room, coursed through her. Before it was too late, she should try to find out what she could from this guy—if there was anything more to tell.

"It would seem that someone doesn't want you talking to us, Mr. Ellis. But so far, you haven't told us anything of real value. Like who hired you. What do you know that is worth your life?"

"I don't know nothing. I promise."

Police cruisers swarmed the parking lot. Now things would get dicey. Would they ask the three of them to come out with their hands up? Given Sawyer's endeavors, he didn't need his name in the news, and she certainly didn't either. Lincoln stumbled forward, holding a hand to his head, and he held his badge high in his other hand so the arriving police would stand down.

He turned and eyed the motel.

Holstering her gun, Everly opened the door and held her hands up just in case someone was trigger-happy. Opening a door while holding a gun was never a way to greet law enforcement. "We're coming out."

Lincoln nodded and turned to the responding officers. "Stand down. The guy who was shooting took off when he heard you coming. I need someone to search the area."

She approached Lincoln and eyed the knot on his head. "The shooter?"

He nodded.

"You should get that looked at."

"I will. He blindsided me, but I'll live."

Thank You, Lord.

"What did you learn?"

"Ellis has confessed to being hired, but he claims he knows nothing more. Someone is trying to kill him, so I assured him he would be put in protective custody if he cooperates."

Lincoln lifted a brow.

"I know, I know. I have no authority to do that, but like you're going to let someone kill him. You're going to protect him, right?"

"Yes."

She stepped back so he could enter the room. Lincoln looked at Ellis, then gave a brief, frowning glance at Sawyer. She hoped that Sawyer would listen to reason and share his full story with Lincoln, a cop he could trust. Lincoln was the kind of guy that might not even put something in a report if harm could come from it. He worked within the boundaries of the law, but justice was his priority. Strong and seriously attractive, Lincoln was an all-around great guy. Why hadn't she ever been interested in him?

But she knew why.

She'd set her heart on the man standing next to Lincoln years ago, and maybe never got over him.

I'm so pathetic.

But now certainly wasn't the time to think on it.

Ellis offered up his wrists. "Cuff me. Keep me safe. I'll tell you what I know."

Which isn't much.

Unless he'd withheld information. At any rate, Lincoln would want to hear it all for himself, though Everly had recorded everything with her cell, though she hadn't gotten Ellis's permission.

A couple of other officers stepped into the room, and Lincoln directed them to take Ellis in for questioning. "Please be cognizant of the fact someone has tried to kill this man today. And that shooter is still at large. In other words, protect him."

He briefly returned his attention to Everly before narrowing his eyes at Sawyer. "We need to talk."

Sawyer visibly bristled.

Oh, come on. Sawyer had to know that he couldn't keep his secrets, especially with the criminal activity surrounding him. To Everly's way of thinking, God had provided the right law enforcement officer in which Sawyer could confide. All Sawyer had to do now was believe it.

Believe and trust.

SIXTEEN

I never thought I'd want this.

But Sawyer couldn't wait to get back to HPS headquarters, a place he'd never wanted to see in the first place. Nor had he desired to stay here. But relief flooded him as he grabbed Layla and hugged her. After a few seconds longer than necessary, he released her, and they strolled down the hallway.

"What happened, Uncle Sawyer?"

"Nothing for you to worry about. I'm just glad you're safe."

He'd been able to contact Brett with Everly's phone and was reassured that both he and Ayden were at the facility. Layla was fine. Everything remained quiet. The bigger issue was that someone would figure out where they were sooner or later or simply follow their vehicle or Detective Mann to the location. But he had also been reassured that no one could get in, and cameras were in place around the facilities.

Yeah...what about drones with cameras? Any cameras watching drones?

But he hadn't asked the question, because they knew much more about protection than he did, even though he was, in a way, also protecting others. Just using a different method. Still, all his clients had doorbell cameras and security systems in their residences, along with corresponding apps on their phones to monitor said cameras and systems, in case their whereabouts were discovered.

In the kitchen Layla reached for a basket filled with snacks—nuts, chips, crackers, jerky. She pulled out a small bag of sour cream potato chips.

"Uncle Sawyer?" She looked so much like her mother, and his heart would break again over Paisley's death if he let it.

"Yeah?"

She popped a potato chip in her mouth and spoke around chewing. "It's cool here. But I want my phone back. My friends are probably freaking out."

And I need to connect with my clients. Everly was supposed to at least give him a burner phone, but he hadn't pressed her. Maybe he should have.

"I need to have a meeting with Everly." And Detective Mann. "I'll ask about communicating with the outside world and find out when we can go home."

Though going home couldn't happen until they had found the source of the problem. And in Layla's case, communicating with the outside world could be dangerous. He'd watched her—after Everly had pointed out her concerns—and he would like to know whom she was texting to make sure it was with appropriate friends. Not someone older. Or a predator.

He really had no response to that. As for the source of their problems, he thought he finally had an idea, but he needed to find out more. "Are you okay?"

"Yes. You don't need to worry about me. It's fun here—and maybe after we get home, I can come back and visit. Shoot hoops with Brett. Hang out with Everly."

"Really." He arched a brow.

"Yes." Her laugh filled his heart. "I started reading *Jane Eyre*. It's a classic. Brett showed me their book-shelves—they have a huge library!—and challenged me."

Layla wasn't a big reader; how had Brett done that? "Well, what do you think of the novel so far?"

"I can't believe I'm saying this, but I'm hooked."

That's probably because you don't have your cell phone to distract you. But he kept those words to himself.

"Well, I'll leave you to finish your chips. I need to talk to Everly. Are you going to be okay?"

"Yes. Quit worrying about me. After I finish the chips, I'm going back to the library."

He turned to exit the kitchen.

"Oh, Uncle Sawyer. Can we have Chinese food to-night?"

"Sure, Layla. Anything you want."

He paused to watch her finish off her chips, then snag a soda from the fridge. She had made herself at home here. He had resisted coming here because he thought it would be a traumatizing experience. The circumstances that had sent them into hiding were in themselves trau-matic, but kids were resilient, and Layla proved that to be true. And being here was turning out to be a good experience for her.

I never would have thought this either.

In all of this…his heart smiled.

Now to find Everly. He found her standing outside double doors, waiting, her chin held higher than nor-mal, and a slight furrow between her brows. When she saw him, the frown slipped away. "You're smiling and I can't figure out why."

He continued toward her and allowed a full-on smile. "I just had the strangest conversation with Layla."

When he approached, he put his hand on her shoulder. "Your brother Brett is amazing with kids. Did you know that?"

"I'm glad she's doing well. We work hard to make sure that if anyone has to stay here for any reason, they have plenty of positive, fulfilling distractions."

He sagged. "Well, I don't suppose that includes me at the moment. Is Detective Mann here?"

"Yes. And waiting for us. Sawyer, you can *trust* him. I've been through…a lot. And he's kept my secrets."

"You have secrets?" About her stalker?

"I have secrets even my brothers don't know."

"And you told Lincoln. I knew there was something between you." Why hadn't he kept his mouth shut? The exhaustion and stress weighing on him caused him to make too many mistakes, and he'd said too much. That was exactly what concerned him about this meeting with the detective she trusted with secrets she hadn't even shared with her brothers.

Or him.

Her frown deepened. He turned and opened the door to the conference room and walked in, hating himself for leaving that conversation, but someone was waiting.

We might as well get this over with.

Trying to organize his thoughts, he slid into a chair at the conference table. Detective Mann was on his cell. Sawyer was half-surprised that Everly's brothers hadn't joined them.

Mann ended his call and nodded to Sawyer and Everly. "I want to know what you learned before I question Ellis."

It seemed strange to Sawyer that Detective Mann had even allowed this, but he and Everly had a special working relationship. What did Sawyer know about anything?

Everly explained what Ellis had said in a concise way.

"I'll send you the recording as well, in case I missed something."

She and Detective Mann both turned their attention to Sawyer.

"Do you have anything to add?" Mann asked.

Before Sawyer could share what he suspected, he would have to tell Detective Mann everything. Or a lot of…everything. He'd worked so hard and long to help others, and he was picking up where law enforcement agencies had failed.

Everly averted her gaze and stared at the table as if disappointed in him.

God, please let this not be a mistake.

"Given that Kevin Ellis's ex-wife has a big attorney from Chicago, it could be a lead for us."

Mann's face remained neutral. "Explain."

"When you question him, find out who her lawyer was."

"I can look into that, but mind telling me why? What is this all about? You've been holding out on me, and I don't like it."

Detective Mann had been patient with Sawyer, and he would give him points for that. Still, he didn't like having to give up his secrets. He stared at the table as if that could give him strength.

"If I tell you everything, and one of my clients ends up dead or their life in an upheaval because of it—" he looked up and stared at Detective Mann "—it'll be on your hands. Mine, too, but you're responsible."

"Are you threatening me?"

"Not at all. I need your assurance that what I tell you doesn't leave this room."

Mann glanced between Everly and Sawyer and released an incredulous huff. "I'm not your attorney. What is this?"

"Just hear him out, Lincoln. I'm confident you'll be more than willing to comply."

Everly and Lincoln shared a look. Sawyer knew the guy liked her in a personal way. It was easy to see.

"And if I can't make that promise?"

"Then we have nothing more to talk about." Sawyer started to stand.

"Wait. If Everly has heard your story… I trust her to know it's worth it. What you share will go no further."

Sawyer eased back into his seat.

Oddly, he wasn't all that relieved to hear that the detective would keep this to himself, because Everly now owed him. What did Sawyer care—he could never have anything with her, and she had made that clear. Even if he wanted it.

He blew out a breath.

"The husband of one of my clients is an attorney in Chicago and also an abuser. She suffered tremendously at his hands. She got restraining orders, but imagine trying to keep safe from a high-powered attorney with connections, including in the Chicago PD. She feared for her life. Her attempts to report to the police or turn him in only ended up being ignored or swept under the proverbial rug."

Acid turned in his gut, but he focused. He had to finish this. "She thought he was going to kill her."

"And? What does that have to do with what's going on?"

Everly leaned forward. "Sawyer makes it his business to protect victims of abuse. He helps them…disappear."

The room fell silent. Apparently, Detective Mann hadn't

expected that news. He angled his head, fairly glared at Everly. He worked his jaw.

Then finally, he said, "I would be interested to hear more details about your business at some point if you need my help or finally trust me. But I don't understand how this connects."

"I admit it seems odd, but if Ellis's wife's lawyer is this same guy, it *can't* be a coincidence. He has the connections and deep-enough pockets to try to take me out. He could have learned that I worked with his wife to help her hide from him."

"But why try to kill you?"

"He hasn't succeeded, so maybe that was never the goal. Maybe it was more intimidating me into giving her up. So that when he finally gets his hands on me, I'll tell him where she is."

Lincoln stood from the table and scraped a hand through his hair.

Everly sent Sawyer a concerned look, then stood too. "The work he does isn't illegal, Lincoln. It's on the up and up. You know that the police often can't do enough to protect someone…someone who is being stalked or is the victim of abuse and afraid for their lives. Women's shelters exist for a reason. Sawyer has offered one more step, one more layer of safety, and a few key individuals within these organizations send certain individuals to him. Those who have no escape from the threat."

Lincoln shared a look with her. "I get it."

Then Sawyer knew that Lincoln "got it" because he knew about Everly's stalker. He hated the sliver of jealousy that spiked through him. He had no right to feel that way, nor was this the time.

Lincoln stood. "Thanks for telling me the truth, Sawyer. I recognize that police reports aren't private and the wrong people can read them and discover who you are and where your clients are. Your information is safe with me. I'll need to be discreet in my questions and in my reporting, but one thing I can't promise is that someone else doesn't discover the truth about the reasons you're being attacked."

And with those words, he walked out, leaving Sawyer feeling like he had just put his clients' lives in danger.

Everly's relief was short-lived. She'd wanted Sawyer to tell Lincoln the truth, but now she shared the uncertainty reflected on his face. Lincoln could only do so much to prevent information regarding Sawyer's activities from getting out, especially if the assailants were linked to the Chicago lawyer.

Sawyer hadn't moved but remained seated and simply stared at his hands on the table. She slowly approached and sat next to him.

"At some point, you must know you've done all you can do, and you have to trust God with the outcome." That wasn't part of their professional mantra, but the Bible verse in the kitchen was a theme.

Do not be afraid. Only believe.

He lifted his dark brown eyes to her, and his expression softened. "I'm glad you have that going for you. I know you're right, but trusting is easier said than done."

She waited but he said nothing more. Time to press. "You clearly have something on your mind. Care to share?"

He frowned and again stared at his hands.

Okay. She would need to talk, and maybe that would get him talking too.

"We can't be sure this lawyer is the man who hired Ellis.

It makes no sense to me. Why try to kill you if he wanted to learn where his wife is?"

"Maybe he has already found her and saw an opportunity to coerce someone into taking me out. Ellis worked the Puget Sound region, which is where I live. That makes sense to me. I need my phone so I can contact my client, the attorney's wife, and make sure she's okay."

"I'll get you the burner phone I promised earlier. I'm sorry about that."

"We've been busy. It's okay. But her number is on my cell phone."

"You can get your contacts off your phone in the Faraday room."

"You have a whole room?"

"Yes, for these kinds of situations."

"That reminds me. Layla wants her phone back."

Everly clasped her hands. "Not surprising. What did you tell her?"

"That I would ask you about it, and I have."

She grinned at that. "You know it's not safe."

"I do. Even if she had another smart phone or a burner phone, which isn't a good idea, she could give away details on social media or to her friends without realizing what she's doing."

"Let's get her cell back into her hands by taking whoever is behind this down."

"Preferably before too many people know about my import-export business."

"You never told me the name of it."

"And with all your protection strategies, you didn't look it up?"

She shrugged and smiled. "I did. You can't be found."

"That's good to know." His turn to smile. "I'm incorporated under BW Global Solutions, and I consult with businesses around the world. I don't move products my-self. I get my business through referrals only—very spe-cial clients. The privacy serves me well."

"It sounds like the perfect setup." She released a heavy exhale. "More than anything, I want to take this guy down. I want to take down all the individuals who have created so much fear. I mean, I can't even imagine hav-ing to give up my life, my home in order to escape abuse and the fear of being murdered."

"But you can imagine it, Everly. How much of your life changed due to the trouble you had?"

"To some extent that's true, but I didn't have to disap-pear as though I was in WITSEC."

He shifted in the chair and looked at her again, that same brooding gaze. "Are you…okay?"

His question surprised her. "Of course. Why would you ask?"

"Lincoln knows about your stalker, doesn't he?"

Again, she was surprised. "Yes. He's the only one. I… never told my brothers."

He stared at her, absorbing that news?

"Why tell him and not your brothers?"

A good question. "My brothers weren't always around." She regretted the words. They could trigger guilt in Saw-yer. "I don't blame them. We were off living our lives. With a judge for a father and an FBI agent for a mother, I come from a strong family with high expectations, even though Mom and Dad are gone now. I wanted to be strong enough to handle things on my own, and…I did." She blew out a breath. "I worked a case while I was with the Tacoma PD, and I had some strong opinions about their handling of a stalker—as in, they weren't really handling it at all. Lincoln asked me what was behind my frustration. I broke down in front of him, and I had no choice but to tell him everything."

"He cares about you as in, he's *into* you. You know that, right?"

She searched his gaze and almost wished she hadn't. Sawyer had always been caring and sensitive to others' needs in a way that most men—her brothers included— hadn't been. At least to her.

"I know."

"Then why are you two not together? He seems like a good man. I can tell you find him attractive too."

Is Sawyer jealous? Wow. Okay.

"Um…" How did she tell him that he'd hurt her and she found it hard to trust anyone not to leave her with another huge gaping hole in her heart?

He suddenly stood. "It's none of my business. I shouldn't have asked."

Sawyer headed for the door.

A pang sliced across her heart. She couldn't let him go like this.

"Sawyer, wait." She rose and moved toward him.

What am I doing?

His hand on the doorknob, he paused, then slowly turned. His half grin appeared forced, or…resigned. "You don't owe me an explanation, Everly."

But she wanted to give him one all the same. "Lincoln and I are just friends."

I made that clear to him just like I made it clear to you. But now the reasons she'd told Sawyer didn't seem so important. Right now, she wanted the feel of his arms around her again. To feel his lips on hers.

Stop it! Stop it. Everly carried too much baggage from their shared past, and Sawyer carried too much of his own—past and present. He would never be in a place to truly love someone.

A sadness filled his dark eyes. "Well, I'm sure he holds on to hope like everyone who fights a losing battle. After all, where would we be without hope?"

Sawyer opened the door and stepped out of the room.

She'd seen something behind his gaze. Was he...*hoping*...for something between them? Or was she imagining the emotion in his eyes, reading him wrong?

Oh, Lord, I'm in trouble. Please, guard my heart.

SEVENTEEN

Sawyer sat in the Faraday room and searched his contacts for Rhianna Kagan, wife of Attorney Ron Kagan of Bartlett Kagan Attorneys at Law. Maybe he was being paranoid. They couldn't be sure it was the same attorney Kevin Ellis's wife used—but it seemed too much of a coincidence for comfort.

Where would he be without hope?

Why had he said those words to her? They were innocent enough, but in saying those words, he'd known he was holding out hope that something would happen between them. He couldn't allow that. He was completely stretched in every direction and absolutely couldn't go through more heartache. Nor could he be the reason Everly was hurt again.

Finally, he found the name. "I got it."

"Okay. I have a cell you can use to call her."

"The problem is, she might not answer if she doesn't recognize the number, so I might need to leave a voice mail."

She led him down the hallway. "Contacting her ties you to her. That isn't an issue?"

"In her new life, no. And if she has been compromised, I probably am too." *Lord, please let it not be so.*

His palms were sweating as he sat in Everly's office

and punched in the number. He didn't think Rhianna would answer, and he left a voice mail identifying himself and asked if she could call him back at this number.

He started to text but hesitated.

"I think she'll call me back if she can. Anyone can easily see a text. I'll wait."

He received a text from a strange number and glanced at Everly, then back at the phone.

I'm scared. I tried to call you.

His heart hammered as he replied,

I can meet you and bring you some place safe until we figure this out. Where are you?

But she didn't respond. Sawyer bolted from the chair and paced the room as he told Everly the news. "It's him. It has to be him."

"All right. Okay. I'll tell Lincoln and see if he has found anything that he could share with the Chicago PD so the man could be brought in for questioning or charged."

"I don't know about this. This could be devastating to more than one client."

Everly rushed over to him and squeezed his arm. "Work on one thing at a time. That's all you can do. This woman must have done something, given something away that allowed her ex to find her *and* you."

"I've put Layla's life in danger with this. What have I done?"

"Pull yourself together. You've helped a lot of people, that's what you've done."

But I still haven't made up for the loss of my sister, of Layla's mother. "I have to go to Chicago."

"What? No, you can't. What about Layla? Your life is still in danger."

"I think… Layla will be fine here with you and your brothers. I'm going to face off with him."

"I don't think this is a good idea. Your business operation to help abused women would definitely be exposed, Sawyer. You're not thinking clearly. I'm going to call Lincoln. I'll let you know what's happening."

She was right. He had to clear his head. Sawyer needed time to think.

Alone.

Everly sounded as if she was dismissing him. Maybe he just wanted her to. He made his way through the maze of the facility until he found the gym. That's what he needed—to burn off energy. Plus, he needed to practice if he was going to shoot hoops with Layla.

An hour later, he was soaking wet. He couldn't believe he'd been in the gym that long, because he hadn't seen or heard from Everly. Just as well. He should get showered and dressed. Half an hour later, he exited his room to go in search of answers.

Everly was striding toward him when her cell rang. She glanced at it, and her eyes widened.

"It's Lincoln. In your room." He opened the door, and they stepped inside together.

"Lincoln, I'm putting you on speaker. What have you learned?"

"You know the saying 'Follow the money'? I put financials on the case early on, and they were able to track the money put into Ellis's account to a holding company connected with Ron Kagan. I've informed Chicago PD, and they're working on it. The issue, as you can imagine, is that he is a powerful attorney, so they're going to want this case to be airtight. Still, they plan to question him, so my hope is that his efforts to harm you or Layla will be shut down."

"Do you trust them?" Sawyer asked.

"I'll monitor the activity, Sawyer, I promise. But there's something else. We don't believe Ellis was working with the men who broke into the house. Of course, he was a target too."

"What if Kagan decided to hire someone to close up loose ends—which only creates more loose ends—but he got nervous that Ellis was going to get caught and say too much?" Everly asked.

"That's my theory too," Lincoln said. "Regardless, Kagan has made a big mistake all around."

"Kind of surprising for someone who knows his way around the law." Everly glanced at Sawyer.

He nodded his agreement.

"But this is how criminals are caught," Lincoln said. "They make mistakes. Even the smartest of them is taken down by their own arrogance."

Everly crossed her arms. "How do we find whoever is still out there trying to get to Sawyer?"

"Like I said, I'm hoping that once Kagan learns we're onto him, he will call off his dogs. He knows what being charged with murder will do to him."

"Lincoln, Rhianna Kagan, Ron's wife, is on the run," Everly said. "She says she's scared, so something obviously happened. We don't know where she is. Her life is in danger—and remember, Chicago PD did not act on her behalf before. Please let us know something as soon as you can so Sawyer can communicate to her. She doesn't trust the police, so there's no use sending them to look for her."

"Understood. Just because Kagan is being questioned doesn't mean that it's safe for Sawyer and Layla to return home or to their normal activities."

Sawyer wasn't surprised by that news.

"But let's see what happens today," Lincoln said. "I'll call you when I learn more."

He ended the call.

Everly blew out a breath and leaned against the wall. "Well, at least we have some good news."

"Yeah. I wish it had been better—as in, they have arrested the man. Considering that he was already committing crimes under their nose, I don't feel very hopeful."

"What happened to your words about holding on to hope no matter what?"

He ran his hands through his hair. "Look, I shouldn't have said anything."

"I know you're frustrated." She looked at him, her eyes warm and…inviting. Then she suddenly lifted her shoulders and smiled. "I have an idea. We have a small in-house theater. Let's watch a movie—something Layla would enjoy—and we can watch it tonight after dinner. Eat popcorn."

"After Chinese food."

"Chinese food?"

"Layla made that special request."

Everly chuckled. "I think we all need a break, and Lincoln is on this. We did the right thing, bringing him in. Don't worry, Sawyer. I'm sure you've taught those you've helped how to protect themselves. Once the threat is extinguished, Rhianna will be safe. We're getting close to the end of this ordeal."

He would put on a good show for Layla's sake, but he couldn't relax until the gunmen were also captured and he learned that Rhianna was truly safe.

God, please help her.

Please help us all.

* * *

The action scene riveted all eyes to the big screen in the HPS small private movie theater. Ayden had truly thought of everything. But Everly couldn't turn off her cell phone. She had to remain attuned to what was going on around them in case an issue arose.

Plus, she hoped Lincoln would call and give them good news.

Her cell buzzed, but looking at it would distract Sawyer and Layla. They both needed the mental and emotional break from the last many days of chaos.

She slipped out of her chair, and Sawyer glanced her way but then refocused on the movie screen. The instant she stepped out into the hallway, the blinking lights and alarms started up.

Caine rushed at her. "Our facilities have been breached."

Everly stepped back as if punched. "What? How? And who?"

"Ayden is in his office, monitoring. You need to get them somewhere safe. Brett and I will take care of it."

"But if someone breached our safe house facilities, where could I possibly take them?"

"You know the drill." His gun drawn, Caine shoved through the stairwell door. "Cops are on the way. Protect your clients."

Everly bristled. She hadn't meant to sound inept, but their facility locations were known to few, and they had never been breached. She raced to Ayden's office and found him loading several guns.

"What are you doing? Please don't tell me it looks this bad."

He glanced up at the security-camera feed on two monitors. "See for yourself."

Two men in tactical gear were making their way through the parking garage. One knelt to set up an explosive—C-4?—to open the doors. Her heart pounded.

This can't be happening.

"We're prepared for every eventuality, Everly. I suggest you secure Sawyer and Layla in the specialized room. No one can get in or out. It's the only way to make sure they're safe until this is over. Put this in your ear."

He handed her the communication device they used in special operations.

She nodded and fled Ayden's office, raced down the hall. Sawyer waited outside the theater with wide eyes, Layla by his side. "What's going on?"

"We have to go. We have a situation." Everly led them back down the corridor."

"What situation?" Sawyer asked.

"I'll explain once we're safe."

Layla whimpered. "I thought we *were* safe here."

"I did too."

She glanced over her shoulder in time to see the accusatory look Sawyer sent her.

"Come with me."

A blast resounded. Layla screamed.

Sawyer picked up his niece and carried her. Everly led them into Ayden's office and through a hidden door behind his bookshelves, then down a short hallway. She opened a thick steel door. "In here. You'll be safe in here. There's a television and snacks and water—and flashlights, in case the lights go out."

She started shutting the door, but Sawyer stopped her. "Wait. You've told me nothing."

"Because I don't know. Now let me join my brothers." She pressed a burner phone into his hand. "Your only contact with the outside world. If someone doesn't open the door in an hour, then call the cops. I'm told they're already on their way."

Her heart hammering, she leaned closer. "It's going to be okay, Sawyer. Will you trust me?"

He pulled her to him and kissed her. Again. "Stay here with us. Please."

"Yes, Everly. Stay with us. I'm scared. I want you to be safe. I can't lose you too. I already lost my mother."

Oh, boy. *Pull on the heartstrings a little harder, why don't you?*

The toughest thing she'd ever done was to step away from these two. "I have to go."

She shut the door before they said more and delayed her further. She crept out from behind the bookshelf and shut the fake walls. Glanced at the monitors.

Gunfire echoed in the hallways.

They had made it this far.

Lord, protect my brothers! Protect Layla and Sawyer.

She held her gun at the ready and moved down the hallway, clearing each opening. A bullet whizzed by, and she backed behind a doorjamb.

More gunfire.

Arms grabbed her from behind in a chokehold, but she delivered a headbutt, freeing herself. She kicked the man in the gut, and he stumbled back onto the floor. Everly stood over him with her gun. "Stay down."

"Everly, you okay?" Ayden's voice came over the comm.

"Yes. I have one of them. How many are there?"

Brett came up behind her, blood oozing from his temple. "Three. We have the other two."

"We've secured the place, Ayden."

"Good. The police are here too."

Everly stared down at the man with the mask and yanked it off. She recognized those eyes. "You were in the woods and then in Sawyer's house. Who do you work for?"

He pursed his lips. He wasn't going to talk.

Lincoln stepped into the room from behind Brett. "I've got this, Everly. Brett."

She blew out a breath and tucked her gun in her holster. "Are we sure there isn't anyone else out there waiting for us to let our guard down?"

"We've secured the perimeter," Lincoln said. He removed the man's additional weapons, cuffed him and then dragged him to his feet. A uniformed officer entered, and Lincoln handed him off.

He turned to look at Everly and Brett. "I was headed this way to give you the news. Chicago PD has a new superintendent, who apparently was itching to bring down Kagan. He was known to be corrupt but had a few cops in his pockets. A lot of others in the city were in his pockets too. They found enough to charge him."

She sagged with relief. "You mean...it's over."

"As far as we can tell since we now have the gunmen."

"I'm going to check on Caine and Ayden, then we'll get Sawyer and Layla." Brett gave Everly a strange look, as if he meant to leave her alone with Lincoln. *Awkward.*

Everly wanted to be the one to open the safe-room door for Sawyer and Layla. They would expect to see her.

But Lincoln stood in her way and stared at her. "When I heard over the police scanner that your facilities had been breached, I was worried about you." He took a step closer.

Oh, no.

She sensed where this might be going. "Lincoln, I..."

He lifted his hand as if he would touch her cheek, then dropped it. "I care about you."

Movement drew her gaze up. Sawyer stood in the doorway, watching, then abruptly turned and walked away.

Her heart sank, but…it was just as well.

EIGHTEEN

Sawyer waited outside the school for Layla, struggling to get back to a normal life. What was normal anymore, especially with Everly's presence no longer needed? His follower and the gunmen had been arrested, and Ron Kagan's bail had been denied.

Rhianna was safe, and she had decided to come out of hiding, as it were, since her husband had finally been caught. She wanted to serve as a witness against him, if asked. Sawyer would be there to help her if things got dangerous again, but it pleased him that—at least in this one case—someone actually got their life back.

And she had wanted her life back. At least she had survived to see this day.

But getting here…

Lord, this was a close call all around. But what do I do now?

He'd thought his calling in life had been to help others, and he wouldn't stop. But he was Layla's protector, too, and he never wanted his job to bring danger so close to her ever again. His job in the past had been the catalyst that moved him far away from his sister. He knew he could have protected her if he'd been here.

Would he ever be able to let that crushing knowledge

go and move on? How many other women did he have to save to feel redeemed? Maybe in the end, only Layla mattered because she was Paisley's daughter. If something happened to her because of him, he would never recover.

As it was, she'd been through trauma he'd never intended.

That, and this morning she'd told him she missed Everly. They had seen her yesterday when they had said goodbye; her services were no longer needed.

He leaned back in his seat and took a deep breath.

Everly.

He closed his eyes.

I miss her too.

But he had not missed the exchange between her and Lincoln. She'd said they were friends, but Lincoln was a much better match for her, and he wanted to be with her. Sawyer should put her completely out of his mind and heart, for her own good. He'd hurt her before, and she'd made it clear that they could not be together.

Ignore the hurt and pain and jealousy.

Hurt and pain and jealousy were often the exact emotions that sent abusive husbands and boyfriends into action.

Sawyer opened his eyes when the school bell rang and got out of the car. He leaned against it, breathing in the crisp air and enjoying a clear day—the first in a good, long while. He'd hired a contractor to fix the broken windows in his house, and he'd spent time this morning cleaning up the mess from the gunfire while Layla was in school.

But he wasn't sure he could live there anymore and had already contacted a Realtor.

He suddenly realized that the buses were gone, as well as the cars retrieving students.

Where was Layla? He texted his niece but got no response.

Then he called, and it went to voice mail.

Panic pinged through his chest, but he calmed his breathing. Sawyer hiked toward the school and up the steps, then buzzed the doorbell. The lock released to let him inside.

The halls were empty.

His palms grew moist.

He rushed inside the school office.

The secretary looked up from behind the large counter. "Mr. Blackwood. I hope everything is okay."

"Where's Layla?"

The woman's face twisted in confusion. "I don't understand. You picked her up earlier today for an appointment."

He fisted his hands. "Clearly, I did not. Where is she, and who picked her up?"

The woman's face paled and she stood. She shuffled through paperwork and files, then pulled out a sheet for him. "This is the form signed by you that Layla presented to us, stating that she would need to leave school early for an appointment."

He stared at the form. That was, indeed, his signature, but he hadn't signed it. He crumpled the paper up. "You need a different system. I never saw this form, much less signed it."

He got on his cell and called 911 and told dispatch that his niece was missing; then he glared at the administrator. "I need to see your camera feeds."

"I'm sorry. We—"

"Don't give me excuses. I need to see what happened when she left."

"Hold on. I'll get security." She rushed away.

Someone buzzed the front doors, but the secretary was away. He rushed around the counter and spotted Everly standing there, looking up at the camera.

He buzzed her in, then raced out into the hall. She ran toward him.

"What's going on?" He gripped her arms. "Why are you here?"

Breathless, she said, "I knew you'd be here to pick Layla up. I had to tell you in person, but I almost missed you, getting here late. I'm glad you're still here. Lincoln called to tell me that Kagan didn't hire the gunmen. There's another person out there. You're still in danger. We don't know who it is yet, but…" She frowned. "Where's Layla?"

He could barely speak past the knot in his throat. "She's gone. She forged a note that she would be leaving for an appointment today. They're supposed to let me see the video footage."

She gasped, absorbing his news. Fear and pain surged in her eyes.

"Use the app that lets you find her cell."

His brain had been too muddled to think of it. He quickly pulled up the app and searched. It said her cell phone was in the school but couldn't tell him exactly where.

Had she left it in her locker, knowing he would track her? He struggled to wrap his mind around the idea that Layla—his loving, wonderful, beautiful niece—would do this.

Next to the secretary, a security guard strode toward them with purpose. Sawyer had to explain all over again what had happened and what he needed. The man quickly pulled up video feed on a computer screen.

The four of them watched Layla head down the steps

with an overstuffed backpack; then she jumped into a black Toyota Tacoma.

Sawyer stumbled back. Found a chair and sat. He leaned forward against his thighs and pressed his face into his hands.

"Who is it? Who did she go with?" Everly asked.

"Put out an Amber Alert," Sawyer said.

"You believe she's in imminent danger?" The security guard asked. "She clearly went willingly."

Sawyer could punch the guy. "Without a doubt."

The security guard got on it immediately, calling a direct contact at the local police department, giving a description and license plate number of the vehicle.

"I'm…so, so sorry," the secretary said. "Please let us know what we can do."

Everly crouched in front of him and pulled his hands down to look into his face. "Who took her?"

He huffed. "'Took' her? Like he said, she willingly went. She planned this. You warned me I should pay attention to her texts, but I didn't listen to you."

He stood and tried to move past the anger that boiled in his gut and the hurt of betrayal. "Layla has left me for Bruce Hughes—her biological father."

Everly gasped. "I thought… I thought he was dead. He's… He's a murderer."

"I thought he was dead too. He was presumed dead since his car had burned up in the crash—but apparently the body inside the vehicle wasn't his because that was him in the driver's seat."

God, how could this happen?

"And Layla doesn't know that he killed her mother. She was young when it happened, and I kept her from the news until all the stories blew over."

Everly hugged him and he held her, absorbing as much comfort and strength as he could from her. He was going to need it.

Everly stood in Sawyer's living room, on the phone with Lincoln. "Through texts and emails, Layla's father convinced her to go with him somehow."

Sawyer paced the room; his stress level had to be shooting through the roof. "Tell him that her father probably convinced her that she had been taken from him, stolen from him. That he'd been searching for her for years."

"Maybe he found you through all the social media surrounding the car accident. We have a lot to work through to figure it all out." She ended the call with Lincoln. "He says he'll be here soon, and we'll work together to figure out where Bruce would take his daughter. But I don't get why he would put her in danger like that. I mean, come on—gunmen in the house? She could have been shot."

"No. I could have been shot, and then she would have been taken," Sawyer said. "Maybe he wanted to scare her out of her comfort zone so she would more freely leave me. Convince her I was dangerous to be around. He'd almost convinced *me* that I was too dangerous for her to be around."

Everly sighed. "I should have told you earlier, but the night the men came into the house, I thought it looked like she had already packed her backpack—that same pack she left the school with. She seemed involved in suspicious texting activity, pretending to sleep, hiding her cell under her pillow. Because I couldn't know for sure and didn't want to cause problems between the two of you, I said nothing more to you after bringing her texting up. I'm so sorry, Sawyer. I should have been more diligent."

He threw his hands up. "There's enough blame to go around, and I don't fault you for anything. Clearly, Layla was deliberate in her actions, and if someone wants to 'run away' with their father, they're going to do it. I didn't want to keep her imprisoned so look where freedom has gotten us."

He paced again and Everly wanted to comfort him somehow. The only way she could was to find Layla.

Come on, Everly, think.

She joined him in pacing until Lincoln showed up, his expression grim, too, as he entered the living room.

"Any news?" she asked.

"We retrieved her cell phone from the locker, but it's locked, and we can't view her messages without her fingerprint."

Sawyer groaned. "I had her set it up with a code so I could, in fact, look at anything if I wanted—but clearly, she changed it. This just gets worse by the moment."

"The phone is with a tech who will attempt to unlock it. In the meantime, we can work on what we know about her father, which isn't much, and try to think of where he might take her. I'm hoping the Amber Alert will help us locate them before he can fall off the grid too far."

Everly closed her eyes. Something gnawed at the back of her mind.

"Everly?" Sawyer asked.

"I might remember something. I only wanted to protect her, and so a few times I caught a glimpse of her texts. Everything sounded innocent enough, including a text regarding camping in Olympic National Park." She opened her eyes. "Do you think she was texting with him and he could have taken her there?"

Sawyer stood up taller; then Lincoln got on his cell.

That was the only response she got. She supposed the national park was an important lead.

Lincoln ended his call and started another, but said, "Someone is going to alert the park rangers to search for them. In the meantime, we're working all angles to find her."

"I appreciate all you're doing, Detective." Sawyer pulled on his jacket and turned to Everly. "Let's go."

"Wait," she said. "You're not planning on actually going there, are you? I have no idea if it's a real clue or not."

"If we think of something else, we'll follow that. But right now, I can't stand here and do nothing. It's as good a lead as any. Layla had wanted to see Olympic National Park, but I hadn't taken her yet. Maybe Bruce took her there. We'll check every single campground. This time of year, some of them will be closing up for the coming winter, so that will limit those we have to check."

After securing her own jacket, she grabbed her things.

"Wait, hold on." Cell to his ear, Lincoln spoke to Everly. "Where are you going?"

"To find Layla."

NINETEEN

The drive to Olympic National Park had taken two hours just to get there; but then adding on the stop and search at various lodges and campsites, plus the two hours Layla had been gone from school before Sawyer knew she'd left… Layla had been missing for eight hours.

Eight hours!

Sawyer just might lose his mind.

"Let me drive for a while," Everly said.

"Can you call Lincoln again and see what's happening on his end?"

"I already called him, and he hasn't called me back. He will as soon as he knows something."

Not good enough. Not good enough!

He nearly missed the switchback on a mountain road and swerved dangerously into the wrong lane. Okay. Maybe he should let her drive.

God, please, help me find Layla safe and sound. But her father wouldn't want to hurt her, would he? Sawyer wanted to hold on to that hope, but he couldn't put anything past a man who had killed his own wife. Well, *ex*-wife at the time, but still. The man was a murderer. Period.

"There's another campground a mile up the road."

"It's cold, wet and rainy. I don't think he's actually

going to take her to a campground. Layla isn't really an outdoorsy kind of person."

"But we should check anyway," she said. "We're here. Let's keep this up."

He scraped his hand through his hair. "You're right."

Adrenaline coursed through him. He had to find her.

"Once I get Layla back—" and he would, because he couldn't consider any other outcome "—I need to radically change our lives."

"I understand. That makes sense. But, Sawyer, isn't that what you did after you and Paisley were kidnapped?"

"Yes. We escaped our father and distanced ourselves from him for a lot of reasons that had nothing to do with the kidnapping. But that was the proverbial straw that broke the camel's back."

"Now, looking back, do you believe you made the right decision?"

"Absolutely." But their escape from their tyrannical father and from the fortune that had put their lives at risk caused other repercussions. Paisley went through an identity crisis. Sawyer believed she'd married Bruce because she didn't feel anyone else would love her. As for Sawyer? He'd moved halfway around the world to get as far away as he could. "The only thing I would change, as you already know, is my move out of the country."

"You can't blame yourself for what happened to Paisley."

Can't I? Her murder was the whole reason he took up protecting women.

"The danger Layla is in now has nothing to do with your business."

"But she was in danger because of me—you can't deny that."

"No, but we handled it."

He turned into the campground. "Are you ready?"

"Yes. We already know he could have switched out vehicles, but we'll look for the Tacoma. Go ahead and park at the campground office. We'll explain what we're doing, show the pictures and ask if they have seen Bruce or Layla. Then we'll canvass the place ourselves."

He shook his head. "The process is too slow." Too painful.

"But we're doing something. We'll get there. We have to trust God."

Do not be afraid. Only believe.

God...help me to believe!

Sawyer pulled his coat tighter as the rain came down. Campers and tents were spread out. Was he slogging through a pointless activity when Layla was nowhere in the park? What Everly had seen in the text could mean nothing at all.

Everly suddenly stopped. Pressed her hand against his chest. "Sawyer," she whispered.

His heart pounded as he tried to see what had triggered her reaction. Night had fallen long ago, and the rain made it even harder to see.

She pushed him back behind a tree.

"I thought I saw Layla go inside that camper. That guy is packing up. He's getting ready to move out. Is that him?"

Sawyer easily recognized the man who murdered his sister, even on this dark rainy night. Fury boiled through his veins.

"You call the police," he said.

Then he started forward and tried to stay behind the trees so Bruce wouldn't go after Layla and use her as a hostage, but his muscles tensed. Everly's repeated calls to come back didn't change his mind.

His footfalls splashed through puddles, and Bruce

glanced up from the open door of the Suburban. His eyes widened as Sawyer rammed into him, knocking him to the ground.

A knife flashed and Sawyer rolled free but didn't escape the slash across his arm, slicing his jacket open. The man scrambled to his feet, and Sawyer met him.

"Where's Layla?" he ground out.

"She's *my* daughter."

"You lost that right after you killed her mother."

"She's better off without her. You took her from me, and now you have to pay."

Rain blurred his vision, along with rage. "You destroyed your family. She doesn't belong with a murderer."

"Uncle Sawyer? What... What are you doing here?"

"Get back, Layla. Stay back. I don't want you to get hurt." Sawyer tried to position himself between Layla and her biological father, who had not been a real father to her.

Would she listen to him? Or had this man somehow turned her loyalty to him because he was her father?

Bruce lunged for Layla, but Sawyer landed a blow to his solar plexus and knocked the knife out of his hand, then tackled him again. "You'll have to go through me."

Sawyer had his hands around the man's throat, squeezing and gripping tighter.

You killed my sister. You're a murderer!

He bit back the brutal words, aware that Layla was too close—but then again, she was also watching her uncle's brutal actions.

Protective actions. He was protecting her.

"Uncle Sawyer, please don't hurt him," Layla said through her tears.

Pain cracked through Sawyer's head when something hit him. Darkness edged his vision. He rolled onto his back, stunned.

No. He couldn't let Bruce take her away.

"Run, Layla, run!" He scrambled to his feet.

The man threw Layla into his SUV and raced around to the driver's side. Sawyer yanked his gun out and aimed at Bruce's head, point-blank. He stood between the man and his escape.

Bruce lifted his hands and started backing away. "You don't want to kill me in front of my little girl, do you?"

"No. But I won't let you take her."

"You're not going to shoot me."

He didn't want to, but Layla was in danger. "Layla, honey? Get out and come over to me."

Layla sobbed, but she didn't get out of the Suburban.

"Don't you dare get out, Layla. I'm your father."

"If you loved her, you would have left her well enough alone." Sawyer ground out the words.

He wished he had held the words back because they had to hurt her. He didn't want to cause more pain. But he would need to end this now. If Everly had called law enforcement, the police, park rangers, whoever was coming, was taking too long.

Bruce suddenly lunged for Sawyer. He was right— Sawyer wouldn't shoot him. Not in front of Layla. Instead, he struck the man in the head with the butt of his gun. Bruce stumbled back. Law enforcement vehicles arrived, lights flashing. Lincoln stepped out of one of them and raced forward, along with park law enforcement rangers, who grabbed Bruce and cuffed him.

Sawyer had never been more relieved to see Lincoln, but… "How did you get here so fast?"

"We got a report the Tacoma had been spotted at Ruby Beach near the park entrance. Brett transported me in the helicopter, but then we heard about Everly's call and I hitched a ride with the rangers."

Sawyer glanced over at the rangers as they ushered Bruce away and into the back of their vehicle.

"You okay?" Lincoln asked, looking Sawyer over.

"I will be." He turned to search for Layla.

Oh, Layla. I'm so, so sorry!

But she wasn't in the vehicle. Where had she gone?

Everly hugged Layla to her.

She'd pulled her from the SUV. The girl shouldn't have been left to watch the conflict between her uncle and her father. She'd already been through so much. Everly sat with Layla in the rental vehicle. Inside, they were safe and warm and out of the rain.

Out of sight of the two battling men. Layla obviously loved her father and her uncle, and the girl had to be torn. She'd been lied to and betrayed by her father and didn't fully understand what had happened. At least, Everly assumed that was the case. When the law enforcement vehicles had arrived and Lincoln appeared, Everly knew that Sawyer would be okay too. In fact, he'd had things well in hand before law enforcement rangers had arrived; but better they arrest the man than Sawyer having to hurt him to protect Layla.

Regardless, at the moment, Layla was alone and suffering. "Shh. It's okay. You're safe now."

"I'm so glad you found me. I… He told me that I had been stolen from him and that Uncle Sawyer took me away from him after Mom died. I thought he was dead. That he had died. He said Uncle Sawyer lied about that. But I heard him on the phone and he…" She choked on a sob. "He was the liar. He was a bad man. I was… I was so scared. But I don't want my father to die. I don't want Uncle Sawyer to kill him. I'm so sorry that I listened to him and didn't trust Uncle Sawyer."

Layla pressed her face into her hands and sobbed, and Everly's heart broke all over again. She rubbed Layla's back, closed her eyes and silently prayed.

Lord, please, please bring comfort into this situation. I have no idea what to do or what to say.

The car door opened, startling Everly.

Sawyer crouched to look in at Layla. She lifted her face from her hands and turned to him. Then went right into his arms.

Relief rushed through Everly.

Eyes closed, Sawyer held his niece—his precious treasure.

Everly took in his handsome face, strong jaw, the blood trickling at his temple. The rain had stopped, or she would tell him he should just get in with them. But she wouldn't interrupt this moment.

Nor would she ever forget it.

Everly's heart was splayed open by this display of love, vulnerable and raw. Selfishly, she wished for a happy ending for herself.

As if somehow hearing her thoughts, Sawyer opened his eyes and looked at Everly, such strong emotion swimming in his gaze that it rocked through her core.

He slowly released Layla and gently urged her back into Everly's arms. "I need to talk to the rangers, and then we can get out of here and go home." He held her gaze. "Are you good?"

As in, can you hold Layla for me?

"Yes." That he trusted her with the job meant the world to her.

She loved Layla too…

Too?

Everly squeezed her eyes shut as pain ignited in her heart. Had she ever stopped loving Sawyer? Maybe she'd buried her love for him so deep that she wouldn't have to feel the pain anymore, but she never actually let go of the love—or of him.

Tears leaked down her face.

Thank You, God, for saving Layla.

Finally, Sawyer returned and climbed into the driver's seat. "Let's go home."

Everly stayed in the back seat with Layla and would hold her for the long ride. Getting out of the park and back to Blue Island would take a few hours, but that meant that Everly could spend those few hours with two people she loved and held dear.

And as for home?

Where was home for Everly? Her apartment would feel more than lonely after spending this time with Sawyer and Layla.

Three hours later, Everly paced Sawyer's living room.

He emerged from the hallway. "She's asleep in her bed. I'll contact a counselor she can talk to tomorrow."

"She's fortunate to have you in her life, Sawyer, after everything she's been through."

"I hate that I couldn't protect her from her father or the truth that he killed her mother." He stared at the floor, a severe frown on his face.

"With your love, she'll be okay. She'll find her way." Everly felt that truth to her core—for herself. Emotion stirred in her chest. "But I think Olympic National Park will be ruined for her for a while. You could take her to Paradise in Mt. Rainier National Park instead."

She shrugged. Now she was just rambling.

Time to go.

I don't want to go.

"Well, Sawyer, I'm glad it worked out. If… If you ever need anything, you know how to reach me."

Everly turned and walked out.

What am I doing?

Inside the rental vehicle, she started it up and drove away.

She was getting on with her life, that's what she was doing. Sawyer had always had so much going on, and it was the very reason in the past he'd walked away from her. Nothing had changed in his life, even though he might have changed. He had no time to put into a relationship.

So she was saving them both the hurt and pain.

She couldn't sleep in her own apartment, so she stayed at the HPS facilities and, much too early the next morning, filled her brothers in on all that had taken place.

"But I'm going home now, guys. I need to get some rest before I start my next assignment next week." Everly drove to her apartment complex three miles away near a peaceful park and lake. She hiked up the staircase to her second-floor apartment.

She shoved aside that dream of a bungalow with a white picket fence, a dog and a cat and 3.4 children. Because, yeah, if Sawyer was her man, then she would have a lot of kids with him. Layla wouldn't lack for cousins to fill her life with joy.

Joy.

She stepped toward her apartment and froze, taking in the strange but familiar sight.

It had been years—seven to be exact—since she'd seen this.

A rose rested on the ground at the foot of her door.

Not black and old.

Fresh and new and red.

Her heart pounded, but she calmed her breathing.

She'd taken care of him years ago. What…what was he doing back? Why now?

Don't panic.

You cannot panic.

Maybe it wasn't her old stalker. But what were the chances she had a new stalker? Whatever. She was prepared to face off with an old stalker or a new stalker, it didn't matter.

She was ending this today.

But…God, why?

Her door was cracked open.

Not shut.

Not locked.

Everly contacted 911 to inform them she had a break-in; then she ended the call. The police were on their way. Police waited for backup. Smart people waited for backup.

But she was tired of the games, and Everly was eager to take down whoever had left the rose and was probably still in her apartment.

Pulling her gun from her holster, she entered her place, sending someone's presence. "I know you're in here. Might as well come out and face me. I've never actually seen your face. Show it to me now."

He'd always worn that stupid mask, the few times she'd caught him. The last time, she was sure she'd broken his nose. She hadn't seen him after that.

Until today.

If it was him.

No one in the living room. Her gun ready, she pressed her back against the wall and carefully cleared the bathroom.

"You startle me and I'm going to shoot you. Come out with your hands clasped together over your head."

"You're not the police," a male voice said.

The sound of it sent spikes of adrenaline through her. In her bedroom, she found him standing there, just looking at her. No mask. She took in the thirtysomething face, dark brown eyes and well-trimmed hair. He had adult acne.

"What are you doing in my bedroom?"

"I love you. I've been waiting on you. Didn't you get my rose?"

"I broke your nose before. Didn't you get my message?"

"I tried to stay away, but I saw you on the news saving a man from a car fire. I knew it was time to try again. We're supposed to be together."

This guy had serious issues.

"Your attention is unwanted. Now the police are on their way."

He took two steps forward, and she fingered the trigger. "Take one more step and I'll shoot."

"I'm unarmed. Are you going to shoot an unarmed man who is only here to proclaim his love? I haven't hurt you. I haven't attacked you. What will your defense be?"

"That you're an intruder."

He lifted his hands. "I'm going already."

But she didn't want him to go. She wanted the police to finally see him and arrest him.

He walked right past her.

"Stay where you are."

"You can't make me." Suddenly, he turned and swung a lamp at her and knocked the gun from her hand.

There you are.

She'd expected the violence to show up.

He flashed a creepy sadistic grin, then lunged for her. She drove her hand into his trachea, and he fell back, gripping his throat. She pushed him to the floor. "Stay down."

The scream of a siren echoed through the apartment. Finally.

"I am never going to love you. I'm sorry you had to ruin your life over stalking someone." Though, truly, love had nothing to do with the stalker mindset.

Love was about sacrifice.

Love was about…Sawyer.

Sawyer was surprised to see the door half-open. In the distance, he heard police sirens rushing to someone in need. He'd heard enough of those to last a lifetime.

"Everly?" He pushed the door open all the way.

She stood over man who was gripping his throat and struggling to breathe. Her beautiful hazel eyes flashed with anger and then widened with surprise. "Sawyer. What are you doing here?"

What *was* he doing here? "First, what's happening?"

"Sawyer, meet my stalker. What's your name?" She pressed her booted foot on his chest. "Oh, you can't speak? That's too bad. You'll feel better by the time the police get here."

Officers entered the room, weapons drawn. Caine rushed in behind them. "Everly, what's going on?"

"This man broke into my apartment and attacked me. He… He stalked me years ago and looks like today he started again."

Caine glanced at Sawyer. "Did you know about this?"

"I figured it out," he said.

But Everly had worked hard to keep that news from her brothers. One officer cuffed the man and started to escort him out of the apartment. "This is a crime scene now, folks. We'll need to collect some evidence, so please clear the premises."

"Wait." Sawyer got in the stalker's face. "I love this woman, and I had better not see your face again. Do you understand?"

The man's eyes widened, but he still couldn't speak. *Whatever, dude.*

He turned to see both Caine and Everly staring at him—in shock at his words?

Caine cleared his throat. "I'm going to talk to the cops, but yeah. It's back to HPS for you, Everly, until they're finished here. But I can tell you two need a moment." He hurried through the door and closed it behind him.

Sawyer had imagined a much different scenario when he'd decided to come to Everly's apartment. She leaned against the counter, and he didn't miss that her hands were shaking, but she smiled at him. "So, what's up? You needed me so quickly?"

This was the wrong time. Why could he never have the right time with this woman? But he'd come all this way, and he would finish what he started. "Didn't you hear what I just told your stalker?"

She shrugged. "You were just protecting me."

Is that what she really thought? This would be harder than he imagined. "You told me that if I needed you, I knew where to find you. But I didn't. I had to ask Brett.

She quirked a grin.

"So you came to find me. What do you need?" Emotion—raw, vulnerable and needy—flashed in her eyes...

And in that moment, he *knew*.

He knew that she needed him too. She loved him too. He wouldn't walk away from that this time.

They had been given a second chance, if only they would take it.

He closed the distance. "You, Everly. I need you."

He pressed his lips against hers, and when she responded, he drew her into his arms and deepened the kiss.

Breathless, he finally ended it, pressing his forehead against hers.

"I love you, Everly. My sister always used to say, 'Life is not about waiting for the storm to pass. It's about learning how to dance in the rain.' That's what I'm trying to do right now. Learn to dance in the rain. I know… I know I bring a lot of drama into things, but please tell me you can give me another chance. Please…dance in the rain with me."

"Yes, Sawyer. I want that chance with you. That dance with you." Everly stepped closer and wrapped her arms around him as though she was ready to begin their dance. "Now we only need a soft peaceful rain."

Warmth and peace flooded his heart. Finally. Sawyer and Everly had their chance.

EPILOGUE

Six months later,
Paradise, Mt. Rainier National Park

Mt. Rainier stood big and beautiful, filling Everly's vision as she held Sawyer's sturdy hand. They strolled along a trail behind Layla who chattered and giggled with two of her girlfriends. She'd celebrated her thirteenth birthday last month and had grown by leaps and bounds in the six months since Everly was back in Sawyer's life.

And part of Layla's life.

She loved him with all her heart and knew that he loved her too. She had wanted to jump headlong into a relationship with him. In fact, if he had proposed on that day he'd declared his love—the same day her stalker had finally been arrested—she probably would have said yes.

But Sawyer was a wise protector of hearts, and he wanted them to take things slowly. Or rather, savor each step in their second-chance romance.

Today, under bright blue skies, they were cherishing each moment and the beauty around them. The joy of God's creation.

And the reunion God had given them.

"Layla, wait up," Sawyer called after his niece.

She and her friends huddled together staring at their cells.

Sawyer stopped and gestured that he and Everly should enjoy the view. She leaned her head against his shoulder.

He slipped his hand out of hers and put some space between them.

She expected him to hold up his cell to take a picture. Instead he turned to her and stuck his hands in his pockets.

He looked nervous.

"What's wrong?" she asked.

"Wrong? Nothing's wrong." He cleared his throat. "Everly...I promise, I won't break your heart. Do you believe that now?"

Did she? Though it had taken time she trusted him not to disappear again. But honestly, she was more than ready to risk a broken heart with this man whom she loved with everything in her. "Yes. I have for a long time. You're a good man, Sawyer."

What was he getting at? Could it be? Emotion surged behind her eyes. Excitement built in her chest.

He dug around in his pocket and pulled out a small box.

Suddenly, Everly couldn't breathe.

He dropped to his knees.

Wow. He was really going to do this the old-fashioned way.

Her mouth fell open.

His expression was filled with love and also terror. She fought not to laugh with excitement as a thrill bubbled up in her throat and at how cute Sawyer was on his knees— nervous and so worried she would turn him down. But she wouldn't say yes until he finally asked.

He opened the small velvet box to reveal a stunning solitaire diamond surrounded by emeralds.

Everly had never seen anything so beautiful and she gasped. Covering her mouth, she stared at Sawyer and the ring.

"I know I blew it before," he said, "but I was messed up after everything that happened. Paisley needed me. But now we have a second chance. At least that's how I see it. I don't want to waste time. It's too precious. We can have a long engagement if that makes you feel comfortable, but I wanted you to know the level of my commitment. Will you marry me?"

"Oh, Sawyer, yes." She let him slide the ring on her finger.

Layla and her friends screamed in delight and took pictures with their cells.

Smiling, Sawyer stood, love shining in his face.

"You love so hard." Her eyes glistened. "So passionately. I think that's why no one else was ever good enough for me after I experienced how fully you love." Tears spilled down her cheeks. "I can't believe that you're back in my life now and actually proposed. That we're engaged!"

Only believe...

* * * * *

If you enjoyed this Honor Protection Specialists book by Elizabeth Goddard, be sure to pick up the previous book in this miniseries:

High-Risk Rescue

Available now from Love Inspired Suspense!

Dear Reader,

I hope you enjoyed *Perilous Security Detail*. Both Everly and Sawyer have gone through so much in their lives that, in the beginning, tore them apart. I'm so glad they got their second chance, and this time, they wouldn't let anything keep them from getting together. I especially love the overall theme of trusting God. *Do not fear. Only believe.* The scripture reminds me of the old hymn *Only Believe.*

> *Fear not, little flock, from the cross to the throne,*
> *From death into life He went for His own;*
> *All power in earth, all power above,*
> *Is given to Him for the flock of His love.*
> *Refrain:*
> *Only believe, only believe;*
> *All things are possible, only believe;*
> *Only believe, only believe;*
> *All things are possible, only believe.*

I hope you find encouragement in the story and in the instructions to "only believe" and trust that God is with you.

I love hearing from my readers, and I invite you to visit my website at ElizabethGoddard.com to learn more about my books, find all the ways you can connect with me and, most importantly, subscribe to my newsletter!

Blessings,
Elizabeth Goddard

COMING NEXT MONTH FROM
Love Inspired Suspense

SHIELDING THE BABY
Pacific Northwest K-9 Unit • by Laura Scott
Following his sister's murder, former army medic Luke Stark becomes the next target when someone attempts to kidnap his son. K-9 officer Danica Hayes and her K-9 are determined to keep Luke and his child safe while unmasking the culprit...before it's too late.

AMISH WILDERNESS SURVIVAL
by Mary Alford
To find her missing brother, Leora Mast must first survive the danger that followed her to Montana. She finds an unexpected ally in Fletcher Shetler...but unraveling the truth behind her brother's disappearance will be harder than she ever imagined. Can they stay alive long enough to save her brother?

TARGETED IN THE DESERT
Desert Justice • by Dana Mentink
After recovering from a murder attempt, Felicia Tennison receives an anonymous message that she has a secret younger sister...and her life is at risk. Now she needs help from ex-boyfriend Sheriff Jude Duke whi'e they seek answers—and dodge deadly attacks.

YOSEMITE FIRESTORM
by Tanya Stowe
Park ranger Olivia Chatham and search-and-rescue leader Hayden Bryant lead a group of climbers to safety from a raging inferno in Yosemite, but killers have orders to destroy all witnesses to their crime...including Olivia. Can Olivia and Hayden get to safety before the flames and killers get to them?

MISTAKEN MOUNTAIN ABDUCTION
by Shannon Redmon
With her twin abducted and mistaken for her, former army lieutenant Aggie Newton must figure out why she's become a target. Together, Aggie and Detective Bronson Young search for answers and her sister, but the kidnappers will do anything to end their investigation.

WYOMING COLD CASE SECRETS
by Sommer Smith
When Brynn Evans learns she was adopted as an infant, she begins digging into her past...and finds a killer intent on stopping her. Brynn's mysterious background is just the kind of challenge private investigator Avery Thorpe can't resist, but is revealing old secrets worth their lives?

LISCNM0223

Get 4 FREE REWARDS!

We'll send you 2 FREE Books plus 2 FREE Mystery Gifts.

FREE Value Over **$20**

Both the **Love Inspired®** and **Love Inspired® Suspense** series feature compelling novels filled with inspirational romance, faith, forgiveness and hope.

HARLEQUIN
PLUS

Try the best multimedia subscription service for romance readers like you!

Read, Watch and Play.

Experience the easiest way to get the romance content you crave.

Start your **FREE TRIAL** at
<u>www.harlequinplus.com/freetrial</u>.